SPOILS
OF THE
DEAD

DANA STABENOW

DANA STABENOW

SPOILS OF THE DEAD

A **LIAM CAMPBELL** NOVEL

HEAD
of ZEUS

First published in 2021 by Head of Zeus Ltd
This paperback edition first published in 2021 by Head of Zeus Ltd

9 7 5 3 1 2 4 6 8

A catalogue record for this book is available from the British Library.
Library of Congress Cataloging-in-Publication Data is available

ISBN (PB): 9781788549172
ISBN (E): 9781788549141

Typeset by Adrian McLaughlin

Printed and bound in Great Britain by
CPI Group (UK) Ltd, Croydon CR0 4YY

Head of Zeus Ltd
First Floor East
5–8 Hardwick Street
London EC1R 4RG

WWW.HEADOFZEUS.COM

For Gerry Ryan, my Irish dad
1933–2019

He would have fallen head over heels for Sybilla

Tikahtnu

Wolverine River

Konstantinovka

Frida Creek

Lake Gruening

Cook's Point

Lightning Cove

Munroe Cove

Chungasqak

Madison Cove

Washington Cove

Blewestown

Jefferson
Cove

Adams Cove

Chungasqak Bay

Chungasqak

State

Mussel Bay

Kapilat

Park

Blueberry
Bay

Maqartuq
Mountain

Chuwawet

Engaqutaq

Arhnaq

Otter Bay

Hot springs ∫∫∫

Park lands

N
W   E
S

0   5   10   15

Miles

Cartography by Mapping Solutions, 2020. Mapmakers.com

But I recognized death
With sorrow and dread,
And I hated and hate
The spoils of the dead.

—Robert Frost

One

Thirty years ago, July

"COME ON, ERIK!" JOSH'S SNEAKERS disappeared over a mussel-encrusted rock ridge left exposed by the low tide. His voice echoed behind him. "We have to get there and back again before the tide turns!"

Like Erik didn't know that. He pulled himself up the ridge, puffing, and saw Josh's tracks in the dark sand, the strides long, the toes dug in. He was running.

Bastard. Erik savored the forbidden word in his mind and even thought about saying it out loud. No one was around to hear, or wash out his mouth with soap, or spank him, or send him to bed without his supper. Which his mother lost no opportunity to do because she thought he was too fat.

Instead, with a heavy sigh, he hoisted himself up over the ridge of rocks covered in barnacles, mussels, and kelp, and slid down the other side to land in the damp black sand on his backside. The edge of a mussel shell had caught his finger.

The wound was bleeding sluggishly, dripping down from his hand. He knew better than to say anything, but he heard Josh laughing, and looked up to see the other boy vanish around the next ridge of rock, his excited voice lingering after him. "Wait till you see, Erik! It is the coolest thing ever!"

It was low tide on an already broad, gently sloping beach that was half sand and half mud, with a narrow section of tumbled gravel between sand and goose grass. The beach stretched down to a glassy calm of sun-washed blue. This side of the bay was backed by two bluffs, one at water's edge and another miles inland. Both were made of glacial silt that had spent epochs washing down Cook Inlet to pack down and pile up, interrupted by seams of black coal. On the other side of the Bay the bright teeth of the mountains gnawed at the lighter blue of the sky. Behind them the summer sun was setting somewhere behind Redoubt, turning the sky toward the pale twilight that passed for night during summer in Alaska. The tide was about to turn and the mud bloomed with a thousand spurts of water, the razor clams digging in beneath the incoming edge of the water. The salt air stung his nostrils and Erik drank it in with every labored breath, watching the shadows lengthen and the light fade. Even at the age of ten he understood that he lived in a beautiful place, and was grateful for it.

"Erik!"

Josh's scream jerked him around in a circle and yanked him into motion up the beach without volition or thought.

"Erik! Help!"

Erik had never heard Josh's voice sound like that, a high, thin edge of fear that knifed right through him.

"No, don't—Erik, help, Erik, no don't please don't Erik help!"

There was the sound of a thunk, exactly like a cleaver coming down on a roast when they butchered out their yearly moose, and Josh was cut off in mid scream.

"I'm coming, Josh! I'm coming!" He tried to run faster but the sand gave way beneath his feet and it was like postholing through deep snow. He rounded the outcropping of black rock, gasping, his chest heaving, his heart pounding so loudly in his ears he couldn't hear anything else but it. "Josh! Josh! Josh—"

There was movement to his left from behind the outcropping and as he started to turn his head to see what it was there was another thud and a kind of explosion of white light followed by a feeling of falling down a deep, dark hole, down, down, down...

And then nothing.

Two

Monday, September 2, Labor Day

LIAM HAD NEVER SEEN SO MANY DO-gooders and no-goodniks in one place at one time. There were only thirty-five hundred people in the city proper and most of them appeared to be either parading or driving down Sourdough Street that afternoon. The marching half held signs and the driving half were harassing them by shifting and clutching at just the right moment during their pickup drive-bys to blanket the marchers with black clouds of exhaust.

Five women who had dyed their hair a matching bubble-gum pink, one hoped temporarily, crossed at the blinking red light where he was stopped. Behind them an older gentle-man punched along on his walker like an AT-AT on Hoth, eyes with sclera aged to the yellow of egg yolks glaring at their backs. His white hair, what was left of it, was sprayed down in a combover whose fixity of purpose was being tested by the breeze caused by the passing traffic. He had a prominent, veined nose jutting from the middle of his face, completing his likeness to an old, bald eagle with acid reflux. At first glance Liam took him for a chronic drunk. Later, upon further acquaintance, he discovered that it was simple choler. Blue Jay Jefferson's factory setting was pissed off.

The blue Forester on his right pulled out and the left-turning Ford F-150 across the intersection slammed on its brakes. No one knew how to cross at a blinking red light anymore. He was glad he was driving his own vehicle and wearing civilian clothes, otherwise he might have had to Do Something. He signaled, counted to three one one-thousand at a time, turned left in the best Gramps Champ fashion, and proceeded sedately down the hill. An actual stop light here, where he turned left again to cross the causeway that divided the man-made lake from the salt-water marsh, accelerated—barely—up another hill and turned left a third time to follow the road to an abrupt corner. There he turned into a parking lot before the road became a four-mile drive out along a spit of glacial silt that thrust out into Chungasqak Bay.

The parking lot fronted what had been a fire station, recently remodeled into a brewpub. Liam parked with care, as his Silverado was brand spanking new and he was protective of its navy blue paint, and got out. A flurry of wings caught the corner of his eye and he jerked around. Only a magpie. He tried not to feel relieved.

The pub was a tall building, with a row of two-story windows on the left displaying rows of shining stainless steel vessels connected by a complicated arrangement of hoses, pipes, and valves. A row of similar windows on the right overlooked the serving side of the brewpub, a wooden bar running the length of the room. Tables and chairs filled up the rest of the space and more windows across the back side of the building overlooked the edge of the bluff, the Spit, and the Bay.

Double doors painted fire engine red occupied the space between the windows. A large, hand-painted sign above read "Backdraft Brew Pub" with a faint hint of flames behind the font. The door opened outward. The man behind the bar said, "We're not open for another hour, Andy, I told you—" He looked up. "Oh. Sorry, Liam. I thought you were someone else."

"An early drinker?"

"We've got plenty of those who'd like to be. As you are about to discover."

He held out his hand. "How are you, Jeff?"

"Shouldn't I be asking you that? How are you settling in?"

Jeff Ninkasi looked to be in his early fifties, with black hair graying at the temples, eyes with an Asian fold that told of his mixed Anglo-Japanese heritage, and a belly that betrayed a love of his own beer. He had lines on his face that betrayed a predisposition for laughter, and the no-bullshit gaze of the professional bartender. You knew just by looking at him that he wasn't about to let anyone drive drunk from his establishment, nor would he allow a woman who'd had a few too many to leave unaccompanied by a friend.

One of the good guys, Liam thought. But then he'd had a week to come to that conclusion, and had already decided that the Backdraft Brew Pub would be where he drank in public in his new posting. Lucky for him the brewmeister-slash-bartender had a full liquor license and already stocked a fine line in Scotch, including Glenmorangie. "How's Marcy?"

Jeff looked up at the ceiling. "Still rearranging the furniture." A thump punctuated his comment.

"I've got that table you said you wanted in the back of the pickup."

Jeff looked sheepish. "Not sure she wants it now. She's decided to embrace minimalism in a big way."

Liam laughed. "Not a problem. Our house in Newenham was small and we left most of our furniture behind. Be a while before we get your house filled up."

"Your house now." Jeff produced a manila envelope from the space beneath the cash drawer of the cash register.

Liam opened it. Inside was the deed and the two-page mortgage agreement the two of them had worked out. "Looks good," he said, and pulled a folded check from his shirt pocket. "First month's payment."

Jeff stuck it in his hip pocket without looking at it. "Thanks. Coffee?"

"Sure."

"Plain drip or espresso?"

"Plain drip's fine." A steaming mug appeared beneath his nose and Jeff went back to drying and stacking glasses.

The coffee was good, hot and strong and tasting like coffee and only coffee. Nowadays too much of the brew tasted burned or, horrors, was flavored with chocolate raspberry or salted caramel. He shuddered.

Jeff noticed. "What? Do you need me to brew up a fresh pot?"

"No, it's fine. Perfect." Liam took another swig. "You don't flavor your beer, do you?"

Jeff looked appalled. "Christ no."

"Because I was loading up on supplies at Safeway yesterday and they had a grapefruit-flavored beer on sale."

"Probably the only way they could get anyone to buy it."

"I know, right? Lime in a Corona is one thing, but..." Reassured, Liam drank more coffee. "There was a parade as I was coming down Sourdough Street."

Jeff rolled his eyes. "Yeah, get used to it, you'll see at least one march every month at this point. And a corresponding parade in opposition."

"What's the difference?"

"The left marches with signs. The right parades with flags."

"What are they demonstrating for?"

"Oh hell, take your pick. Today's Labor Day, so probably unions. Traditional, okay, but tomorrow it might be the Tea Party, Antifa, Black Lives Matter, hashtag MeToo, save the sea otters or the whales or what the fuck ever. This is the wokest town in the state." He brightened. "But marching is

9

thirsty work evidently, because most of both sides show up here afterward."

"Silver lining."

"Yeah." Jeff racked a tray of glasses and started on another. The door opened. "Hey, Jeff."

"Hey, Erik. We aren't open yet."

"I know, but I was hoping you could sell me a growler of Cockloft without sending the ABC board into convulsions."

"That I can do. Wait one."

A man about Liam's age, tall and rangy with thick, wheat-blond hair and sea-blue eyes leaned against the bar. He nodded at Liam. "Hey. Erik Berglund."

Liam nodded back. "Liam Campbell."

"Archeologist." Berglund volunteered the information like he expected a fanfare of trumpets in response.

Liam was interested, though. "Oh yeah? Here on the Bay? What have you found?"

"Save yourself, don't get him started," Jeff said, reappearing with a brown ceramic jug that would have been more at home at an Appalachian hootenanny.

Erik grinned, unabashed, and handed over his card. "Harpoon heads, arrowheads, axe heads, fish hooks, a bone drill, frames for dip nets, stone oil lamps, and what I think are the pieces of a snare."

"A snare for what?"

"Fur-bearing animals, I think." Erik shrugged. "I'll know more once I manage to figure out how it goes together."

"How far back do they date?"

Jeff groaned, handing Erik his card and receipt. "I'll pay you a hundred bucks to take back that question."

"I will make you eat those words, Ninkasi."

"Will you make Domenica Garland eat them, too? Because you'll have to."

Erik winked at Jeff. "She's already given it her best shot. She didn't leave happy."

"Oh, man, you turned that down? Hell, I'd tap that!" Jeff cast a nervous look at the ceiling. "I mean, I would if I wasn't married."

"Uh-huh." Erik tucked the jug under one arm. "Also, not what I said." He grinned when Jeff's eyebrows flew up. "Come see my dig… Liam, right? I'm up the Bay twenty miles, on the Bay side of the road. It's a steep climb down but I promise it will be worth your time. Thanks, Jeff. Later." He was out the door with a backwards wave.

"Oh, shit," Jeff said.

"What?" Liam turned to see Erik pause briefly before another figure, also a man. "What's wrong?"

Jeff came out from behind the bar fast and hit the door before it had closed fully behind Berglund, Liam right behind him. By the time he caught up with Jeff, a third person had pulled up in what looked like Lincoln's ne plus ultra version of a Navigator, black in color. The woman that slid down from the driver's seat was a looker, medium/medium, but with her weight distributed in a manner that would have made Rubens weep. Her waist-length hair was nearly the same color as her vehicle and she wore jeans and T-shirt to match her vehicle and so tight that you could eyeball her pulse through the cloth. As much-married as Liam was he was also a man and it was difficult to drag his eyes up to her face. When he did manage it his gaze was caught and held by a pair of large, dark, widely spaced eyes whose initial Disney-princess look was belied by an intelligence so sharp it might draw blood. How much was up to her, and if you got in her way.

"Dom," Jeff said in a resigned voice. "To what do I owe the honor?"

"Just starting the day off right, Jeff." She made even that innocuous statement sound seductive. She strolled over to stand next to the man confronting Berglund. A more unlikely couple would have been impossible to find. She was perhaps in her early forties and he looked at least twice her age and a quarter her weight. She stood erect, shoulders back, those amazing breasts thrust out in front of her like bazookas taking aim, skin glowing with health and vigor. He was thin to the point of emaciation, stooped over a chest caved in by age, all exposed skin freckled with liver spots, only wisps of colorless hair remaining in the barest fringe above his ears. His eyes were red and watery with swollen lids and his right hand was curled arthritically over the head of a massive diamond willow cane with a braced handle that looked as if it weighed as much as he did. His remaining energy was directed in what could only be described as a homicidal glare at Erik Berglund. His voice was high and raspy and vicious. "You ignorant lout, you puppy, you—you—" Spittle flew as the old man spluttered to a halt.

"Hey, old man," Berglund said, impervious. He gave the woman a long look, head to foot, and his mouth curled up on one side. "Domenica. Looking good, as always."

She gave as good as she got, a sultry once-over that made Liam glad it had passed him by because he was afraid of what would have happened if it hadn't. "Erik." She turned to the older man. "Leave it, Hilary. Erik's, quote, findings, end quote, will never hold up. No point wasting your energy in a quarrel that will never go anywhere. RPetCo needs you in fighting form for when we get to court."

Liam was standing a little behind and to the right of the group and he could see everyone's expression but Jeff's pretty well. He saw Erik's lethal grin flash out at both opponents impartially, and there was a broad chuckle in his voice when he replied. "Whatever makes you sleep better at night, Dom." He winked. "I'm always, ah, up for that."

Dom, or Domenica, was not one to be outfaced or even the least little bit embarrassed. She smiled back at Berglund. Jesus. Liam hadn't seen such a blatant come-on since watching J.Lo strip on screen. "I seldom repeat myself, Erik."

Erik's beam edged into a knowing smirk. "More than three or four times, anyway."

Dom slid her arm through Hilary's and urged him past Erik and Jeff. "About opening time, isn't it, Jeff?" She caught sight of Liam and paused, infinitesimally, but it was long enough for Liam to feel an interest that was as searing as it was brief. He found himself blowing out a breath after she had passed by and looked up to find Berglund's knowing gaze on him. "Careful there, dude. She will eat you alive."

"I'm a married man," Liam said.

"Keep telling yourself that."

It took a moment for his vision to clear completely and when it did he saw the old fart with the walker was a step behind the old fart with the cane. He glanced at Liam in passing and slammed to a halt. "Trooper."

"Yes, sir."

"Recognized you from your photo. Blue Jay Jefferson. I'm kind of a fixture in these parts."

"Sergeant Liam Campbell. Nice to meet you, sir."

"You were the cop who figured out the prop murder," Jefferson said. "Tricky." He held up his left hand. The middle finger had been broken between the first and second joints and healed crookedly. "Made that mistake once myself. Easy enough to do when you're not paying attention."

Liam wondered what Wy would say when he told her that.

"You're out of uniform," Jefferson said.

"It's at the cleaners in Anchorage," Liam said.

"Hey, Blue Jay." Erik saluted Jefferson with the growler, hopped into a dusty Ford F-150 old enough to be carrying its own cane, and chugged out of the lot.

Blue Jay Jefferson stomped past with his walker to Backdraft, where the woman was holding the door open for him.

"Who the hell is that?" Liam said.

"I'm guessing you mean her," Jeff said, heavy on the irony. "That's Domenica Garland. President and CEO of RPetCo Alaska."

"Oh." It was a weak response and Liam knew it. Trying to recover some portion of the genitalia that had followed Domenica Garland into the brewpub, he said, "Who are the old farts?"

Jeff sighed. "The one who was foaming at the mouth is Hilary Houten. Also an archeologist. He and Erik have, ah, professional differences. Blue Jay Jefferson is so far as I know the oldest living inhabitant of the Bay who was born here, white or Native. He knows where all the bodies are buried, including the ones he buried himself." He changed the subject, by chance or design Liam couldn't tell. "What does your wife think of the house?"

Liam thought of the three-bedroom, four-bathroom house on the edge of a 600-foot bluff that overlooked even more of the Bay than the brewpub did. "She'll see it today."

"My wife would have killed me dead if I'd bought a house before she'd had a chance to look at it."

Liam smiled. "If it's clean and warm and there is hot water, Wy will be fine with it. She cares more about what she flies than where she sleeps."

"That's right, you said she was a pilot." Jeff cocked his head. "Commercial?"

"Bush. Owned her own air taxi in Newenham. Sold up when this job came along."

"When does she get here?"

Liam looked out the window at the clear skies beyond. The Bay was flat as a skating rink. "This afternoon, if the weather holds."

And if Wy hadn't changed her mind, again, and turned around halfway.

Three

S HE HADN'T.

She was taking her time, however. Leaving behind the place where she'd lived much of her life and owned and operated a successful business had not come easily. When Liam had been offered the job in Blewestown they had half-heartedly discussed the possibility of a long-distance marriage. She was a pilot, after all, with two paid-for airplanes with her name on the titles, one of which, if she pushed it, had a cruising speed of upwards of a hundred fifty mph. Liam's new posting was only about two hundred fifty miles from Newenham, less than two hours in the air in the Cessna, wind and weather permitting.

Not that she would push it because of the wear and tear on the engine, but in the end, neither of them could face the time apart. Newenham had changed on them, too, and recent events made leaving sound more attractive than staying.

Her adopted son, Tim Gosuk, was *déjà vu*, at AvTec in Seward, a town a hundred fifty miles from Blewestown with an actual paved and maintained highway connecting the two, a rarity in Alaska. His current proximity to Liam's new post was another incentive.

She was still smarting from the sale of Nushugak Air Taxi, though. Fifty percent of small businesses failed by their fifth year. Hers had not failed, it had thrived, and she was leaving behind a decade of experience and goodwill to begin cold somewhere else. It was not an attractive prospect.

Housing in the Alaskan Bush was always at a premium and commanded what one might kindly term extortionate prices, but she wasn't ready to sell so she rented her house to a young couple from Icky who said they were ready to move into town. Wy suspected it was more about them escaping the too-attentive eye of their relatives, most of whom lived in Ik'iki'ka. She had relatives in Icky, too, and she knew how that went. The husband had a job working road maintenance for the state and she worked at the hospital and Wy knew them to be good people, so she signed the lease and arranged for the rent to go into her account at the local branch of First Frontier, which she also kept open. No harm in keeping all her bases covered, she thought. She didn't mention it to Liam. Not that he ever asked. He was pretty smart that way.

It startled her, when it came time to pack, to realize how little she had in the way of personal property. Almost everything she owned was business-related, from the two planes down to her tools, pilot handbooks, aircraft manuals, work clothes, and four survival kits, winter and summer times two, one for each aircraft. Her photographs were on her phone. Her only jewelry was her wedding ring and a pair of diamond stud earrings and she never removed either.

What she owned more of than anything else was books, and those she had packed and shipped. She downloaded the Kindle app to her phone and filled it with favorites and to-reads to tide her over until her books appeared in Blewestown. Since they would travel by barge to Anchorage and then by truck to Blewestown, that wouldn't be tomorrow. Her music had already been transferred to iTunes. Everything else she packed into 68 Kilo and lashed it down with cargo nets. 78 Zulu was already in Blewestown, ferried there by a Newenham pilot Wy trusted who had family in Cook's Point.

Her last night she walked through the little clapboard cottage, looking to see if she had missed anything. Liam had bought a house fully furnished in Blewestown and she was renting hers the same way, which was going to save on freight. Everything had worked out so smoothly she was inclined to be a little suspicious of the whole process, because nothing in her life had ever been this easy before. She walked out onto the deck that reached the edge of the bluff and stood looking out at the great river, gray with glacial silt that made it look like a flow of molten lead moving rapidly toward the sea. A fish jumped and smacked back into the water. Probably a late silver.

She would miss this view, and this deck. Here it was that she had practiced form with her grandfather, Moses Alakuyak, almost every morning. Without thinking about it she dropped down into horse stance, feet shoulder width apart, knees bent, spine straight, arms bent at the elbows, palms cupped to face inward, body weight centered. Root from below, suspend from above. Without her willing it her limbs flowed into commencement, ward off left, right push upward, pull back, press forward, push. Below, needles rattling, a porcupine with the rolling walk like a drunken sailor characteristic of her species trundled into the middle of a dense patch of high bush cranberries and began to eat her way out again.

Moses had strong-armed Liam into form on Liam's first morning in Newenham, and in memoriam to that diminutive, irascible old shaman the two of them continued to practice together each and every morning they woke up in the same place. Moses was gone now, killed by a stray bullet, one of a swarm of bullets loosed by an idiot who had no business anywhere near firearms, and, too late for Moses, never would be again.

Fist under elbow, step back and repulse monkey, slanting flying, raise hands, stork spreads its wings. Bill was gone, too. Bartender extraordinaire, local magistrate, longtime lover of Moses Alakuyak, and one of Wy's few really close friends in Newenham. Bill had sold her bar the month after they buried Moses and made good on a lifelong threat to move to New Orleans. She had written to say that she'd bought a townhouse two doors down from the Terminator's terminator. There had been no second letter so after a few months passed Wy had had Jim Wiley, Liam's geeky friend in Anchorage, track down Bill's phone number. Bill had answered on the first ring. She'd sounded pleased to hear from Wy but said she was on her way out the door to her new job tending bar. She name-dropped at least three Marsalises and one Neville, explained the Terminator reference, and hadn't called back.

A vee of Canadian geese flew past, honking steadily, heading south to join up with other flocks at the mouth of the river. There they would spiral up into one gigantic flock and peel out south for warmer climes. It was a sight Wy looked forward to every year. Perhaps she would get a glimpse of them when she took off in the morning.

Left brush knee and twist step, needle at sea bottom, fan through the back, turn and white snake puts out tongue. A pair of eagles chirped and warbled at each other from adjoining treetops. One of them, as if in punctuation, lifted its tail and squirted a rich stream of yellow poop, just missing a parky squirrel. The squirrel said what he thought. The eagles responded with what sounded a lot like laughter, although Wy told herself she was anthropomorphizing. Something Alaskans often did as a matter of course, seeing as they were surrounded by wildlife designed by nature to eat them first chance it got. They were easier to live with if you ascribed human behavior to them.

Pull back, press forward, and push, single whip, all four

fair ladies working at shuttles, and back into ward off left and through to push. As it always did the form steadied her, calmed her, focused her. Root from below, suspend from above. Her muscles loosened and stretched, supple, elastic, strong. She sank into single whip creeps down and stepped up to form seven stars. The chi that Moses had told them lived behind their bellies held her steady over her own center of gravity. That belly that would never hold a baby.

She took a deep breath and let it out slowly. Retreat to ride tiger, turn round and kick horizontally, shoot a tiger with bow, step up, parry and punch. She may have put a little extra into the punch. Apparent close up and conclusion as the light faded above and the river rolled inexorably on.

She repeated the entire form twice more, commencement through conclusion. At the end she straightened, brought her right fist into the palm of her left hand, let her hands fall to her sides, and bowed, deeply. Respect for the form. Respect for the sifu. Respect for Moses. She blinked back tears and went inside.

In a gift to the last fishermen and the first hunters of both seasons a high had settled in over Southcentral Alaska from Bristol Bay to Prince William Sound on the Friday before Labor Day, and took up residence for the foreseeable future in NOAA's ten-day forecast. Wy woke very early on Labor Day to clear skies, visibility unlimited, and light, variable winds out of the southwest. The winds were included, she thought, only because the forecasters couldn't bear to give out a perfect weather report. If she'd submitted a request to the weather gods to facilitate the quickest, smoothest, cheapest, least wearing on the engine flight from Newenham to Blewestown, this would have been it. It was almost as if the fates were conspiring so that she had no excuse not to get in the air and put the nose on east-northeast.

She put the sheets in the washing machine and did form on the deck until it was time to put them in the dryer. She showered, dressed, and did a final walk-through of the house. She carried a small duffel to the door and locked it behind her, and then had to unlock it again in a scramble to find the current book, the third in the kickass Gunnery Sergeant Torin Kerr series. She only wished she was that tough. And then she locked the door again and left the keys for Zach and Alexis on the highest shelf inside the arctic entry.

They'd sold their vehicles because the price of shipping them from Newenham to Blewestown was more than a new vehicle would cost them—another advantage of being on the road system—and she drove her rental to the airport, and turned it in. The girl behind the counter was unknown to her, a relief because she'd been dodging goodbyes for the past three months. They all thought she was running away, and they weren't entirely wrong, but the sympathy touched her on the raw. Best just to be gone. Like Bill, she'd write.

Or not.

She had topped off the tanks the previous afternoon. All that was left to do was the walk-around and to run the checklist. She let 68 Kilo use up most of the runway and they took to the air over Newenham for what might well prove to be the last time. She made a large, slow circle as she climbed, the Wood-Tikchik Mountains to the north and west, the Four Lakes parallel streaks of silver reaching deep into the mountains, the wide river rolling down to Bristol Bay in the south, the town itself spread out over the hills and hollows of the broad north bank of the river, surrounded by thickets of alder and black spruce. The town of Newenham was always more attractive from a thousand feet up.

She banked right and headed east, following the river up just far enough to fly over the spot where Old Man's Creek joined it. Moses' fish camp was still there, although the cabin looked even more dilapidated than it had the last time she'd checked on it. The Arctic was hard on everything.

"Goodbye, Grandfather," she said, and was surprised and perhaps even a little forlorn when her eyes remained dry. It seemed she was leaving the worst of her grief at her loss behind her, too.

She banked right, climbing again, leveling out at five thousand feet, and put Carly Rae Jepsen on the soundtrack. Wy preferred real instruments to synthesized but the girl had pipes. She followed the river up to where it petered out into braided lakes and tundra, crossed the Kvichak and emerged onto the southern shore of the massive Iliamna Lake and proceeded up the east shore. There was a tiny bit of chop for about a nanosecond and then, poof, gone. Wy wished Liam were along for the ride, just to prove to him that every flight in Alaska wasn't a death-defying feat on the order of a shuttle launch. How she had managed to fall for a guy who held up in the air every aircraft he ever flew by the arms of his seat remained a mystery to her. A reluctant smile spread across her face. To both of them.

The lake was a bright sheet of glare beneath the rising sun. There no sign of the infamous albeit elusive lake monster to be seen over the entire seventy-seven mile stretch, which was disappointing, but she did catch a brief glimpse of some of the lake's freshwater seals. She'd read that there were only two freshwater seal populations in the world and that predation, pollution, and climate change was eating at their numbers to the point that application had been made to classify them as endangered. She had very little faith left in the government doing the right thing so she was happy to see them while she still could.

She followed the dirt road from Pile Bay over the mountain pass to Williamsport on Cook Inlet, mostly because she had heard stories for years of death-defying transits over that road. She had herself never seen it, so she dropped down until she was about eye level with a pickup that looked way too small to be hauling a fifty-foot fishing boat on a trailer up a track barely wide enough for the wheel base of both vehicles. It made her glad she was traversing the pass by air. Even more so when that track was halfway up a dizzyingly sheer mountainside with nothing between the edge of the road and the abyss and oblivion.

She climbed back up to cruising altitude and flew on. Over the headphones she heard sporadic communications from various pilots in the area, picking up and dropping off guests at fishing lodges, spotters looking for late schools of silvers, a bunch of hunters en route to harvest their share of the Nelchina caribou herd. The Alaska Department of Fish and Game had increased the hunting season by ten days as the latest estimates had the population of the Nelchina herd at fifty thousand plus, which was about twenty thousand over what the area could sustain. Wy had flown aerial surveys for the ADFG and she had seen up close and personal what happened when herds over-grazed their ranges. Malnutrition and starvation weren't pretty in any species.

Iliamna Bay passed beneath, a long stretch of gold on blue. She banked left at North Head and maintained a heading just off shore for the circumference of Iniskin Island, with Iniskin Bay and Oil Bay passing in review. For a few heart-stopping moments all four stratovolcanoes lined up on either side, a stalwart line of ice and granite. Douglas, seven thousand feet; Augustine, forty-one hundred feet, an island volcano, an almost perfect white cone floating in a dark blue sea; Iliamna, ten thousand feet; and Redoubt, also ten thousand feet. Spurr, eleven thousand feet and the fifth in line on the west side of Cook Inlet and nearest to Anchorage, was visible, too, if much less spectacular in appearance after its peak-altering eruption in 1953. They formed the northern thrust of the Aleutian Range, a two-thousand mile arc of mountains beginning at Lake Chakachamna west of Anchorage and ending with the Rat Islands at the tail end of the Aleutians. This was the northernmost arc of the Ring of Fire. These five mountains would be her guideposts to the south and west for the foreseeable future.

The fact most prominent regarding these mountains—What was the collective noun for volcanoes? An eruption?—was that they were all active and in the habit of sending ash high in the air and hundreds of miles in every direction, rendering a severe hazard to aviation. She eyed Augustine attentively as she approached it but it seemed calm today. On her left Iliamna showed steam from two vents, as did a single vent on the west side of Mt. Redoubt north of it. South of Augustine, Douglas bestrode Cape Douglas, a protrusion of the Katmai National Park. Katmai was where the tourists who could afford it flew in to watch bears and where the Apollo astronauts had trained for survival, although NASA would have had to work awfully hard to put a capsule down that far off course.

"The shoulders of giants," she said out loud, and indeed the massifs seemed to be holding up the blue dome of the sky itself.

She followed the long, wide gravel beaches of the west side of Cook Inlet north, pausing at Silver Salmon Creek to circle around a pair of grizzlies digging for clams in the mud left by the outgoing tide, skirting the inner shore of Chisik Island to fly part way up Tuxedni Bay just so she could say she had stared Redoubt in the face, then doubling back to bank left over Squarehead Cove and Redoubt Point.

At Harriet Point she banked right and flew out over the vast blue expanse of Cook Inlet, her new home.

Four

Monday, September 2, Labor Day

LIAM WAS A SINGLE MALT SCOTCH MAN BUT on his way out of the brewery he bought a growler of Firebreak Lager to support a fellow local. He stowed it in the cooler behind the driver's seat of the Silverado and stood for a moment, irresolute. He should go home and finish unpacking. Although he had made the bed, which was the most important thing. It was his sincere hope that the bed would desperately require clean sheets in the morning.

As if she'd heard him his phone buzzed with an incoming text from Wy, in which she ETA'd him that she was about ninety minutes out, followed by two emojis, a heart and a flame. His heart skipped a beat, because of course it did. Liam Campbell was that greatest of all clichés, a man truly, madly, deeply in love with his wife, and he didn't care who knew it. What's more, he was loved just as much in return, and he didn't care who knew that, either. He could feel his swagger coming on just climbing into the truck and he was positively cocky turning the key. Even if he was laughing at himself just a little bit as he did so. Ninety long minutes, he thought, as the engine idled. How far up the bay had Erik said his dig was?

A shadow passed between him and the sun and he almost felt rather than heard the susurration of wings. He looked up. It was only an eagle, wing tips feathering the air, white head and tail almost erased against the pale blue of the sky. The likeness to Blue Jay Jefferson was even more pronounced. Not a raven, though, so all was well.

He put Brad Paisley on the speakers, turned up the volume, and drove back across the causeway that separated the lake and the tidal estuary, where he turned right on the road that led east out of town. Imaginatively named East Bay Road, he noticed. In spite of there being a hundred times the number of road miles and five times the population of Newenham, he had the feeling it wasn't going to be all that difficult to find his way around Blewestown and environs.

Near to town, the road was paved with large shoulders, a center turn lane and, if his eyes did not deceive him, an actual bike trail, on both sides no less. About five miles out it intersected with another road that led back around to the airport, named, in another excess of creativity, Airport Road. After that the road devolved into a narrow corridor of mixed residential and business, with the trees crowding in on both sides, especially thicket after thicket of alder and a lot of dead or dying evergreens. The spruce bark beetle was still single-mindedly pursuing its determination to eat every last spruce tree in North America, made manifest here by stand after stand of spruces that had died and turned from deep, dense green to dull, tattered brown. East Bay Road was one lightning strike away from a raging forest fire that could wipe out everything from here to town, and Liam wondered why the dead trees weren't being cleared. He rounded a corner and saw a crew with a cherry picker taking down one such stand as he passed by, a tall, once-proud tree crashing down in a small cloud of dead needles shaken loose by the impact.

He watched his odometer and at about twenty miles out, after a deep dive into a ravine carved by a small creek crossed by a very old wooden bridge and a switchbacked climb up the other side, he found a driveway on the right. The street sign had been knocked into the ditch but he could make out the letters. Glacier View. He looked across the Bay, where an enormous glacier, all swirling white and blue and gray and black ridges, curved down between two mountains to preen over its reflection in the still water beneath. Glacier view, indeed.

The driveway was so steep it almost disappeared in front of him, a single lane dirt road that followed the narrow creek he had crossed. He passed several smaller driveways to the left and right. Just before the driveway ended there was another driveway off to the right. This driveway was in infinitely better condition, wide enough for two cars to pass and maintained to an excellence seen only on the other side of the Alaska-Canada border. It turned after fifteen feet, losing itself in the alders clustered thickly on either side, but there was a large roof with a handsome rock chimney looming up over the foliage.

Past the driveway the lane became even steeper with ruts that went so deep Liam feared even the Silverado would high center. After two switchbacks thrown in just to slow down the traffic, the dirt road mercifully ended in a small turnaround about a hundred feet off the beach. The beater Erik Berglund had been driving was parked far too close to the edge. A weathered post indicated where there might be a trail down, if one were suicidally inclined.

Well. God hates a coward. He parked and got out. He stood for a moment, looking out at the Bay. The blue expanse seemed to stretch out even farther the more he looked at it, though he knew it was only twenty-five miles wide and forty miles long. Distance over water, like sound, was deceiving. The fact that he was law and order for everything he saw that wasn't muni meant he'd be flying a lot. Joy.

He walked over to the post stuck in the dirt. Sure enough, it indicated the top of what could only in jest be called a trail. Pushki, that tall, noxious Alaskan weed whose juice could blister the skin right off your body, crowded a steep gravel slide interrupted by needle-sharp black rock outcroppings and ending in a small but murderous ridge of that same rock thrusting out onto the beach itself. For a brief moment Liam debated just how badly he wanted to see Erik's dig. He sighed and shrugged. He was here, Wy wasn't due in for another hour. What the hell.

He inched forward, almost immediately lost whatever traction he started out with, and began to slide. He hit the first outcropping of rock, tripped, barely caught himself before what would have been a truly epic face plant, skittered over the gravel rolling beneath his soles, hit the second outcropping, and flailed his arms trying to regain his balance. Failing, his feet slid out from beneath him and he sat down hard on the trail, which wasn't any kinder to his jeans than it had been to the soles of his shoes. He might have yelled. He certainly didn't scream like a little girl. He slid down the rest of the way on his butt, working up enough velocity that he only narrowly avoided impaling himself on a sliver of rock extended invitingly from the ridge that protruded onto the beach.

He climbed gingerly to his feet. Bones intact, only a few scrapes and bruises. Nothing that Wy couldn't kiss all better. He hoped no one had been photographing his ignominious descent with a cell phone. Although it would certainly have been quite the clickbait.

"Hey! Liam!"

He looked around.

"Up here!"

The creek he'd crossed ended in a stream that spread out over the beach in a wide fan. On the trail side time or tide had carved a cave into the rock, leaving a more or less level bit of shelf behind. Erik Berglund's head poked out from the flap of a white canvas tent. He was grinning. "You believe in making an entrance, don't you?"

Liam investigated the seat of his jeans. The fabric might be a little thinner that it had been at the top of the trail, but fortunately denim was tough stuff. "It was a little more exciting than I had anticipated. You ought to post a warning sign."

"I could, but what would be the fun in that?" He waved. "Come on up."

Liam looked at the steep tumble of rocks, which to his eyes looked freshly spewed from a volcano, and sighed again, but it was nothing compared to the trail and shortly he was standing next to Erik at the door of the tent.

Three sides were rolled up halfway. The fourth side faced the cave and was rolled up all the way to the top and securely fastened with twine. There were fold-out tables, a folding stool, and various bits of paperwork, including a roughly drawn map, pinned to the canvas just beneath the roof. A foam bed was folded in thirds, topped by a rolled sleeping bag and a small duffel.

Erik followed his eyes. "Sometimes I bunk down here."

Liam, thinking of the access trail, could see why. The tent was big enough for Liam to stand up in, which as a tall man he appreciated.

"Welcome to my lair," Erik said with another wave of his hand. "Depending on who you talk to around here, I'm bringing truth and justice back to this part of the world, or I'm figuring out how to end resource extraction in the entire state. Which of course means an end to the world as we know it."

"Wow. You must be powerful."

Erik laughed. "You and I have no idea."

"So, not a dig, but a cave."

Erik nodded. "Yeah, I found the cave and explored. There is a natural shelf inside on the right, high up. It looks and feels planed to me, which could have been either deliberate or caused by usage. Either way it supports my thesis. Another thing?" He turned and pointed. "You see the way the rocks on the top of the spur look a little flatter and smoother than normal?"

Liam followed Erik's finger. "I guess?"

"Trust me, it's there." Berglund dropped his arm. "This is the only significant spur of rock on this side of the Bay north of the Spit. I think the old folks, the Alaska Natives who made a living out of the Bay before we white folks were born or thought of, used this site as a small harbor to access the interior of the Kenai Peninsula."

Liam digested this in silence for a moment. "Why not just use the Spit?"

"There wasn't any harbor on it back in the day, and therefore no shelter from the big storms, not if they wanted to leave their boats there while they were trading in the interior. There isn't much shelter on the Spit now, come to that. Next big quake and whoosh. But here, they would have had the Spit as a barrier between them and the big swells and the high winds." He turned and faced the cliff and pointed upward, although they couldn't see anything through the roof of the tent. "I think this trail is a lot older than everyone thinks today. There's a creek, a small one, that zigs and zags all the way up and over the bluff."

He nodded to the left and Liam saw water trickling out of a gap in the cliff. "The driveway follows it down."

Erik nodded. "I haven't walked all of it but what I've seen so far suggests a foot trail that follows the creek and climbs all the way up and over the back bluff. From there they could have traveled to portages across Tustumena and Skilak Lakes and on to trade with the tribes in Kenai and Soldotna."

Liam scratched his head. "Why not just take their boats around? The Alutiiq were seriously good at long distance rowing. Baranov used them to get around."

"Ah, but if they went around they'd miss trading with all the people along the way."

Liam shrugged. "It's a theory."

Erik laughed, unoffended. "I'm buying a drone to take pictures from the air. Next summer I'm walking the trail until I lose it or it loses me. There are traditional trails all over Alaska. The Chilkoot and the Iditarod are the most famous but they aren't the only ones. You know the old Iditarod starts in Seward, right?"

Seward was on the eastern side of the Peninsula and considerably farther north. "Yes."

"I don't want to theorize ahead of my data, but I'm hoping this trail connected with that one and I'm hoping to find proof of it."

"How far back do you think this trail goes?"

"How far back did the first Alaska Natives get here?"

"That's a long time for a trail to last."

"Trails don't just disappear. They get overgrown and flooded out, but they never completely disappear. Look at the Roman roads."

Liam looked toward the trail. "Not exactly Roman engineering, there."

"Trails don't just disappear," Erik said again. "If it's there, I'll find it."

"What happens if you do?"

"I used to work for UNESCO. If I can find enough to prove my theory, I can start agitating for them to consider making the trail a World Heritage Site."

Liam was impressed and showed it. "You mean like the Grand Canyon?"

"More like Taos Pueblo or Mesa Verde. Man-made."

Liam looked out at the drill rig parked in plain view, and wondered what RPetCo thought about Erik Berglund's ideas.

"You ever seen a dig site before?"

"One."

"Really?" Erik looked and sounded surprised. There probably weren't many people who responded to that question in the affirmative. "Where?"

"Outside Newenham."

"A Yupiq site? I don't—oh. Des McLynn?"

Liam nodded. The archeological community in Alaska couldn't be so large they wouldn't all know or at least know about each other.

"What an asshole."

"Agreed."

"What were you doing there?"

"Investigating." Liam waited. This was always the turning point in meeting new people. A lot of cops called those they were sworn to serve and protect "civilians." He preferred "neighbors" himself, but he'd found that he'd had to prove himself in every community in which he'd served, and that his job lost him a lot of friends from the moment they became aware of his profession.

"That's right, Blue Jay called you a trooper."

Liam nodded.

"Wait a minute," Erik said. "Newenham. You're that guy. The Storyknife Killer."

There were many ways Liam could have answered but he settled on, "Yes."

Erik shook his head. "Murder by archeological artifact. That's not a headline you see every day." He jerked his head. "You want to see what I've got going on here?"

Liam relaxed. "Why I defied death getting down here. You said at Jeff's that you thought human habitation went back farther in the Bay than is generally understood."

Erik snorted. "Yeah, mostly because archeologists just don't fucking listen."

"Listen to whom?"

"The people who lived here first, for starters."

"Alaska Natives, you mean?"

"The Sugpiaq locally. Aleuts or Alutiiq they're better known by, but their own name is Sugpiaq. And then the

Russians showed up and of course that's where all the history books start." He shook his head. "*Littera scripta manet.*" He saw Liam's blank look. "The written word survives. It's pretty much the only thing that does. Why we get Homer forced down our throats in high school."

"I remember," Liam said, with feeling. "So, you're saying because the Sugpiaq didn't have a written language—"

"Exactly."

"So there's no written record there was a trail but—"

"Exactly," Erik said again, beaming.

"Have you asked them? The Sugpiaq?"

"Not yet. I'd like to have some concrete evidence before I do."

The guy was so excited that it was hard not to like him. "Where is your evidence?"

Berglund grinned. "Trooper," he said without heat.

Liam grinned back. "Guilty as charged."

"Too much to eat not to have," Erik said. "There was a monograph written by Hilary Houten—the old fart you saw yelling at me at the brewpub, he's not a fan—anyway, Houten wrote a paper thirty-odd years ago that claims the lack of artifacts proves that no one settled here, or at least on this side of the Bay. Well, maybe they didn't settle here, but they sure as hell used it." He stood in front of one of the tables, where many unidentifiable objects were neatly laid out and labeled. At least half the names on the labels were followed by question marks. "This is for sure a harpoon head—see the barbs? No flies on the old folks when it came to building something that would hang on to what they stuck it into."

"Arrowheads?" Liam said, pointing.

"A bunch of them. If I can get them dated I might be able to work up a decent timeline, but you can see the evolution of the technology, stone to iron to stainless steel." He grinned. "I admit the metal ones don't exactly help prove my thesis, but it does show that the locals have been using this cave for a long time. These are axe heads."

"What's that groove?"

"Where they tied it on to a handle. See where the twine or rope or whatever crossed over?" Erik was practically glowing with excitement and appeared delighted to share his expertise, and Liam warmed to him. People who liked their jobs were the luckiest people in the world, and by far the most fun to talk to. "Those shaved areas are where they shaped the striking edge with another tool."

Even Liam could recognize a fish hook when he saw one, but Erik had discovered one carved from wood that was as big as his hand, flat with wicked-looking barbs.

"For halibut," Erik said. "You'll see stainless steel hooks almost exactly like that on a halibut boat today."

"If it ain't broke don't fix it."

"Exactly." Pleased, Erik nodded his head. "This is that snare I told you about."

To Liam it looked like a jumble of old bones, although he could see in places where they had been shaped by human hands. For what purpose, he had no clue.

He turned to look at the Bay. The rock outcropping extended out at least a hundred feet and was almost exactly perpendicular to the bluff that edged the beach. Nothing but sand on either side. Good bottom for landing a boat. The location was halfway between the head and the mouth of the Bay, so reasonably accessible to anyone living on the other side, especially experienced seamen like the Aleuts. He looked at Erik. "How did you find this cave?"

The archeologist's smile faded, but he said readily, "A friend and I were beachcombing around here when I was a kid. I remembered the outcropping, and since it's such an anomaly on this side of the Bay, I thought I'd take a look."

"Lucky guess."

"No kidding." Erik's voice was flat. He dropped one of the snare parts and shoved his hands in his pockets. "It would be something."

He spoke in such a low voice that Liam was not sure he was meant to hear. "What would be?" he said.

"If I pull this off. If I find proof. It would be something to give. Something to leave behind. Do you have kids, Liam?"

"Two," Liam said. Charlie might have died but he was never gone to Liam. "You?"

"I'm told it makes you think differently about things."

"It does." Liam pointed. "Is that a rock hammer?"

"Yeah. How'd you know?"

"*Shawshank*."

Erik laughed. "Good movie."

"Any movie with Morgan Freeman in it is a good movie.

I would have thought the last thing an archeologist would need is a hammer. You're all about the not breaking of stuff."

"It's not mine. I found it here." He gestured. "With the rest of the artifacts."

Liam picked up the hammer. The head was rusty and the paint had faded from the handle.

"Erik!"

They both looked up as if trying to see through the top of the tent.

"Erik? You down there?"

"Hey, Gabe!"

"You got company, I see. You mind more?"

Erik laughed. "Not that kind of company, Gabe. Come on down."

A cascade of small stones preceded the visitor, who maintained a lot more control over his descent than Liam had. Probably only because he'd had more experience.

"Who's Gabe?"

"He's just my neighbor up the hill." Liam was pretty sure he was holding back a smile.

Liam remembered the big roof and the stone chimney. "Ah. Your landlord?"

"Sort of, but not really."

"Cryptic."

"I try."

A pair of long jeans-clad legs appeared beneath the top of the tent and both men turned to watch as the owner of the voice galloped down the incline and jumped the last four feet of the trail to land neatly on the beach, the impact scattering gravel and sinking him ankle deep in the sand. He punched the air. "And the crowd goes wiiiiiiiild!"

Erik laughed and the third man turned and grinned at them. "Hey, Erik!"

"Hey, Gabe! What brings you down the hill?"

"And a slalom of a hill it is, too. Who's your friend?" He squinted into the sun.

"Liam. New to town. I met at him Jeff's this morning when I went in for a growler. I told him about the dig and he came out for a look."

Gabe walked forward to get under the tent and out of the sun. "Nice to meet you, Liam." He stuck out a hand.

"And you, Gabe."

He tried to let go of the handshake but Gabe held on. "Wait a minute. I know you."

"We have met." Liam had recognized him immediately but he had not expected to be recognized in turn.

"I'll say. In Newenham. Sergeant Liam Campbell."

"That would be me."

"You still a trooper?"

"Yep. You still a movie star?"

"Yep."

They both laughed, and Gabe McGuire, Oscar-winning action film star, breaker of a billion hearts and a bona fide box office bonanza, turned to Erik and said, "We met in Newenham, what, two years ago now."

"Almost. Still have that FBO in Chinook?" Liam said.

A shadow crossed McGuire's face. "Sold it. The lodge, too."

The FBO at least had some Erland Bannister DNA so Liam could understand it, but still. "Damn. Sweet properties, both of them."

Gabe smiled. Usually you couldn't see him acting, but today wasn't his best effort. "Too much baggage." He spread his hands. "And hey, I'm a Bay boy, now."

Erik snorted, and Gabe laughed. "Reason I came down is, I'm throwing a little watch party this evening. I'm inviting all the neighbors. Booze and I've got hot dogs and hamburgers for the grill, and six different kinds of ice cream for after."

Erik laid his hand on his heart and let it thump a few times. "You had me at booze, but Dom, too?" Gabe rolled his eyes and Erik snorted again. "Like you wouldn't tap that."

"Seriously, dude? That woman comes with her own freight train of baggage." He turned to Liam. "You're invited, too."

"Thanks, but—" He looked at his phone. "I've got just about enough time to get from here to the airport to pick my wife up when she lands."

"The hot pilot, right?" Liam raised an eyebrow and McGuire grinned. "I'm not blind. Bring her along."

"I'll ask her," Liam said, knowing he would do no such thing. He hadn't seen Wy for a week and what he had in mind for the evening didn't include an audience.

Gabe read his expression. "Yeah, never mind. Rain check."

"Works." He looked at Erik. "Thanks for the tour."

"Anytime."

"I'll follow you up," McGuire said.

The way up was arduous but less death-defying. They stood at the top for a moment to catch their breath. "You get this view from the house?" Liam said.

"Oh, yeah."

Liam looked towards it but the trees were impenetrable. "How long have you been here?"

"Almost a year."

"Buy or build?"

"Bought. Some dot-com gazillionaire built it, spent about twelve days in it, and decided it was too far from the nearest server farm." Liam laughed and Gabe smiled. "Seen anything of that FBI agent or that reporter?"

"Mason and Dunaway? Dunaway's always in and out on stories. I've talked on the phone to Mason a time or two." Liam looked at him. "Did I remember to thank you for giving Kate Shugak a ride back from Adak that time? I still owe you for that."

Gabe shrugged. "I can always use more hours in the G-2." He shoved his hands in his pockets and looked away. "I was real sorry to hear."

"Hear what?"

Still not looking at Liam, Gabe said, "That she died."

"Who died?"

McGuire did look at him this time, clearly annoyed. "Kate Shugak."

"What?"

"You didn't know? I thought Alaska was the original seventh grade classroom, everybody knows everything about everybody else."

"Kate's not dead, Gabe."

"She got shot. I heard. Her and that monster dog of hers, too."

"True," Liam said, "but she didn't die. Monster dog, either."

McGuire stared at him. "Kate Shugak's alive?"

Liam got the feeling McGuire was tap dancing but he couldn't figure out what around.

"I was told she was dead," McGuire said slowly.

"Who told you that?" McGuire didn't answer, and the answer dawned. "Erland Bannister? Your business partner in Newenham?" McGuire looked away and Liam said, "Yeah, well, he actually is dead. And never a man whose word you could trust when he was alive, by the way." Liam checked his phone again. "I gotta book."

The one-lane dirt road was just as awful going out as coming in and he achieved the paved surface of East Bay Road again with the feeling of having dodged an enormous repair bill. McGuire could afford to turn that poor excuse for a road into the Champs-Elysées, so why put up with what was basically a hog wallow?

A second later he answered his own question. Why would Gabe McGuire of all people want to make it easy for anyone to come visit?

Mystery solved, he headed back into town with a heart

that lightened with every mile. He was already smiling when he turned left on Airport Road, and he was positively grinning when he entered the code to get through the gate onto the field. He drove to Wy's tie-down and got out. The sun was warm on the back of his neck and he stood there for a moment, enjoying the place, the day, the anticipation of greeting his wife in his best Duke of Marlborough imitation.

Perhaps just to remind him that all joy is conditional and fleeting, his brain brought up the images of Jenny and Charlie, his first wife and their son, both killed by the same drunk driver. That event had begun a downward spiral that had nearly destroyed him mentally and emotionally, and very nearly professionally as well. That spiral had culminated in his being assigned to the post in Newenham, a location so remote and a town so lacking in all the mod cons they couldn't even keep a city cop on the payroll, never mind a trooper.

But there he had found Wy again. He looked at the image of Jenny's face in his mind's eye and saw her smile at him. They had been such good friends, and generous woman that she was she would never have wanted him to live out his life in loneliness and misery. She would have been happy he had found Wy again, and again, he hoped with all his heart that she had never suspected the affair. Jenny had been and always would be the best person he had ever met in his life, and this far on the other side of his loss he knew he was all the better for having had her in it.

It was harder to look at Charlie, even in his own imagination, to see again that soft, tiny bundle of gurgling charm blowing bubbles at him, those tiny fingers grasping his own. Sometimes Liam's arms actually ached to hold his son again. His heart did ache at the loss and always would.

He heard the distant drone of an airplane and looked up, squinting into the sun.

Five

Monday, September 2, Labor Day

STRETCHING ALMOST TWO HUNDRED MILES from the city of Anchorage to the Gulf of Alaska, the vast estuary called Cook Inlet was host to tides second only to those off the Newfoundland Banks, as well as some of the best salmon fishing in the world. Wy crossed the southernmost tip of Kalgin Island and continued on a southeasterly heading, to cross the coast of the Kenai Peninsula at Tikahtnu, a town of a thousand people perched on a bluff divided by a river and its tributarial creek.

That bluff began in Turnagain Arm in the north and continued west and around and all the way down the west side of the Kenai Peninsula and up to the head of Chungasqak Bay which, as she rounded Cook's Point, unfolded before her in all its forty miles of glory. She studied up on it in advance but nothing could have prepared her for the disparities between the north and south shores. The north shore was almost agricultural-looking, a broad bench of mostly flat land between a short bluff at water's edge and a much taller bluff farther inland. The south shore looked like Norway, where a range of sharply pointed, white-capped mountains slid precipitously into slivered eighty-fathom fjords. The fjords alternated with five massive piedmont glaciers, themselves depending from a seven-hundred-square-mile ice field only the mountains held in check. Between the fjords were small, rocky inlets and bays and coves and lagoons, along with the occasional spit, tongues made of millennia of glacial silt washing down Cook Inlet. The largest spit thrust out four miles perpendicularly from the north shore. A handful of islands lined up in front of two of the larger fjords on the south side, with a few more so small they could more properly be called rocks scattered by an indiscriminate hand.

Liam's first reaction to being offered the job of the new trooper post in Blewestown had been to dive into the crime statistics in the area. Wy had hit Naske and Slotnick's *Alaska: A History of the 49th State*, the *Alaska Atlas & Gazetteer*, Merle Colby's *A Guide to Alaska: Last American Frontier*, one of the state guides published by the Federal Writers Project back in the day, and of course her personal copy of AOPA's Airport Directory. She glanced at the clock on the dash, and on impulse turned right to follow the spit across the Bay for an aerial tour of the south side. The longer this big high hung in over Southcentral, the bigger the first fall storm would be that was certainly building up behind it in the Gulf of Alaska. If you don't like the weather in Alaska, wait ten minutes.

She'd been making a slow descent since Tikahtnu and now she leveled out at a thousand feet, maintaining a course that held just offshore, watching and listening for traffic. There were half a dozen airstrips in the various villages and towns on the south side of the Bay, and where there weren't airstrips at low tide they used the beaches. She checked the tide app on her phone. Low tide was just an hour away. She grew the extra pair of eyes that all good pilots held in reserve for situations like these and proceeded with enough caution to avoid a mid-air collision but with enough attention to appreciate the view. Over the headset she heard pilot chatter from three different aircraft; from Chuwawet (taking off), Beaty's Hot Springs (landing), and Jefferson Cove (humpback cow and calf alert). The Chuwawet pilot announced his ETA for Blewestown, which prompted a brief but incendiary blast from someone on the ground in Engaqutaq who apparently had passengers and freight waiting for transport to Blewestown. No reply from the pilot, although the resulting silence on the channel was electric with expectation, everyone muting their mics in the hope of hearing the Engaqutaq ground crew tear the pilot who had changed the schedule mid-flight a new one.

Wy grinned and drifted west, the throttle up just enough to keep her from falling out of the sky, giving her time to peer up every nick and notch big enough to admit a tide. The mountain peaks held up almost to the very end of the peninsula but there was no level ground to be seen afterward, just multiple rough granite slabs off the vertical by only a few degrees. Two different collections of islands, one close in about five miles offshore and another about ten miles further south and sixty degrees more to the west, looked just as horizontally challenged. There wasn't a cove big enough to spread a beach towel on or a place flat enough to land even a Super Cub. Maybe there was somewhere to land on floats but she wasn't on floats today. She circled and headed back up the south coast of Chungasqak Bay.

The nineteen-hundred-foot airstrip at Blueberry Bay was built on a gravel spit that separated a lagoon from the Bay, attended by a few dozen houses and cabins scattered between the water's edge and halfway up the nearly vertical hillside the airstrip dead-ended in. Not a strip she would take for granted, not without multiple touch-and-goes for practice first. The community consisted of 103 people and was according to the last census a hundred percent Sugpiaq, although it had originally been a Russian fort under Alexander Baranov's tenure as Catherine the Great's Alaska exploiter-in-chief. Recently the citizens of Blueberry Bay had unilaterally reclaimed the settlement's original Sugpiaq name of Chuwawet, and were now in the process of convincing the US Postal Service they had the right to call themselves what they wanted to and still have their mail delivered.

Deeper into Blueberry Bay, Engaqutaq had a two-thousand-foot airstrip on a hill the top of which had been sliced off specifically for the purpose. Black spruce clustering menacingly on three edges as if just waiting for the starter's pistol to sound before they reclaimed their territory from its two hundred residents. The edge closest to the water was lined with—she dropped down for a look, and then circled back for another look. Yes, those were headstones. Engaqutaq had a cemetery off the edge of its airstrip.

Most of the houses in Engaqutaq paralleled the strip, the way Alaska villages had been built in the old, more sensible days, when all you had to do was hop out of your plane and walk across the strip to get to your front door. After statehood the FAA had brought in a bunch of federal money and most of the airstrips had been relocated to five or ten miles out of town, among other things introducing allegedly better aids to navigation, along with the unintended consequence of wheeled vehicles, not to mention driver's licenses, to the Alaskan Bush. Engaqutaq had originally been a US military fort of much more recent origin than neighboring Chuwawet's Russian fort, rapidly succeeded by a herring cannery and then, when the herring were fished out, a salmon cannery, astonishingly still in operation. Wy had thought that all salmon were fresh frozen nowadays.

She dropped down to fly low and slow at a hundred feet above the strip, and even on this clear, calm day there were thermals enough to raise a few bumps. It would be an interesting approach in real weather. A couple of kids ran out of their houses and waved furiously. She waggled her wings and was up and over the ridge to the east, which revealed a much longer, narrower body of water forcing its way far more deeply into the Kenai Mountains. According to the chart this was called Mussel Bay, Wy assumed for the obvious reason, with a small town perched on its northeast shore.

Kapilat was a comparatively substantial community of three hundred people, with a summer population that filled the vacation homes built on pilings along the opposite shore, some of which harbored pretensions of McMansion status. The mountains rose around the narrow bay in four-, five-, and six-thousand-foot knife-edged peaks clad in an omnipresent layer of ice and snow that grew or receded with the season. Above the head of the bay their snowmelt emptied every summer into a small river whose flow had over the millennia carved a cramped chasm with multiple narrow falls alternating with gravel beds created by the moraines of retreating glaciers.

Wy banked left and turned back down the bay, coming down to a hundred feet to take a look at the airstrip. Like all the other strips on this side of the Bay it was unattended and unpaved, two thousand feet carved out of the side of a foothill with a salt water slough paralleling it. There was no traffic so she dropped down for a touch and go. As in Chuwawet the thermals made themselves felt, but the surface was well-maintained and there were half a dozen hangars, which she would bet belonged to the McMansion owners on the other side of Mussel Bay. She lifted off gently at the other end and banked left over a road on a dike that divided the slough from another slough that debouched into the Bay proper. She climbed back up to a thousand feet and debated her course. There was much more of the south shore to explore, the chart showing multiple tiny coves and narrow bays and shallow lagoons.

But across the Bay, Liam waited. Across the Bay was Blewestown, a community of ten thousand people spread along the Sterling Highway from Cook's Point to the Wolverine River delta that formed the easternmost end of the bay. Blewestown's primary reason for being was the afore-mentioned four-mile gravel spit, a spit that had been washed clean by the tidal wave that followed hard on the heels of the '64 quake and was therefore, so to speak, open for business. From the sale of Alaska to the US in 1876 to 1960, Westerners had been trying to make a living in and around Blewestown without much success. There was gold, but nothing to com-pare to the Klondike or Nome. Fox farms and cattle ranches came in with fanfare and failed in obscurity.

The biography of the town's namesake had made for an entertaining read. George Blewes had been the third lieutenant on *HMS Endeavour* when Captain Cook sailed into the now eponymous Cook Inlet. In 1896 his descendant, Albert Owen Blewes, of whom report held that he never walked a straight line where a crooked one was available to him, began his career in his native land with multiple petty thefts while he was still at school. Returned forthwith to his appalled parents, he continued with the selling of legal documents proprietary to the London solicitor to whom he was apprenticed, embezzlement of the shipping firm where he was later, albeit briefly, employed, and an illegitimate child. This last had evidently been the proverbial straw, as immediately thereafter his family handed him a one-way ticket to New York and did not wave their tear-stained handkerchiefs from the shore as he sailed from Southampton, off to make his fortune in the New World. Wy wondered what had happened to the child.

In New York City, Blewes spent his first year in America leasing land in Wyoming to which he held no title. Fortuitously for Blewes, right about then gold was discovered in the Yukon and like all good confidence men of that day Albert yielded to its siren song and lit out for the territory of Alaska, by all accounts one step ahead of the bloodhounds. In Dawson City, sticking to what worked for him, he made a fair bit of money leasing gold prospects he did not own. As was his invariable habit, he beat feet out of Dawson one step ahead of the law, arrived in Nome to spend just enough time for Wyatt Earp to issue him a blue ticket south, and rode Alaska Steam down and around the west coast to the Kenai Peninsula, where in 1910 he was put forcibly ashore in Chungasqak Bay for nonpayment of gambling debts. Later he claimed that the voice of his lauded ancestor had called out to him from the very shores.

Always a charmer, as grifters invariably are, he managed to raise enough of a stake to buy most of the land at the head of the spit and much of the spit itself, after which he created a real estate prospectus filled with beautiful pictures and exclamatory phrases like "Thick stands of virgin timber as far as the eye can see!" and "Land so fertile it will support any crop!" He talked himself aboard the next Alaska Steam ship bound for Seattle and took a train back to New York City where, against the better judgment of all the people who remembered him from his last visit, he sold everything he held even partial title to in Blewestown and much that he didn't. The only thing he left behind was his name on the town, because certainly he never saw it again.

For the next hundred years the prospectors and fox farmers and the cattle ranchers came and went, while the fishermen came and some of them stayed, but Blewestown remained the Bay's stepchild, no more than a fuel stop for the steamships who put into the one dock, where the tracks of the little railroad which began in the coal seams of the bluffs ended.

And then in 1960 the highway was built, and the 1964 earthquake destroyed the infrastructure of Kapilat, and Blewestown's fortunes began to rise in almost exact proportion to the falling fortunes of the communities across the Bay. The Blewestown Chamber of Commerce website listed a dozen halibut charters, almost thirty restaurants, and over a hundred bed-and-breakfasts, attesting to its place as a tourist destination for locals and Outsiders alike. There was a thriving arts community, including painters, potters, and a musical population big enough to support a chamber orchestra, a jazz band, several rock bands, at least a dozen folk music groups, and an annual music festival that brought musicians in from all over the state and all over the country. A local luthier hosted workshops in building stringed instruments to apprentices from all over the world. There was a fifty-bed hospital and half a dozen clinics, four dentists, three veterinarians, and—Wy counted—two coffee roasters and six coffee shops if you included the drive-throughs. There was even a Starbucks. In the local Safeway, but still. For someone coming from a town of two thousand with no road, this was big-city living with style.

Along with tourism and the arts, Blewestown was the market town for the Bay, where everyone came to buy food, building supplies, and get their hair cut. The mirror image, in fact, of Kapilat sixty years before. There had to be some feelings about that locally.

Wy saw the humpback cow and calf she'd heard the chatter about. They were swimming a lazy circle, until they passed into water cast into the shade by the mountain next to it. With a sigh she left them behind and set a course for the tip of the Spit.

It was a twelve-minute flight from Kapilat to Blewestown, following the string of islands off the south shore before turning left to catch the tip of the Spit and follow it inland. A drilling platform sat on three legs halfway up the Bay. At this distance it looked only parked, not in operation.

The Blewestown airport (so dignified because it had an intermittent ATC presence and was paved) was seven thousand feet long. Under "Obstructions" the AOPA directory warned of moose and seagulls. Since birds were the bane of every Alaskan pilot Wy kept her head on a swivel. She saw a bald eagle and a five-member flock of sandhill cranes but no seagulls and thankfully no moose during her descent.

The airport consisted of a commercial hangar on the north

edge, deserted at present because the latest in a string of fly-by-night commercial carriers had filed for Chapter 11 and stopped regularly scheduled service between Blewestown and Anchorage from one day to the next. A distance down the apron was an FBO, a fixed base operator, servicing privately owned aircraft. Today it had a small jet parked next to it, a Gulfstream, she thought.

The south edge was lined with private hangars and two that belonged to two air taxi services, which made absolutely no sense, as people flying in from the south shore communities would then need transportation to go all the way around the airport to catch a flight to Anchorage. It probably had to do with the federal dollars used to build all US airports. Nonsense in Alaska always came back to the requirements placed on the spending of federal dollars there.

There was also a seaplane base on a shallow lake that paralleled the runway, host to several flightseeing services. That much she saw before 68 Kilo kissed the tarmac of Blewestown Airport's in a runway paint job. She let the craft run out of steam with only a gentle application of the brakes—there was plenty of room, after all—and when 68 Kilo had slowed down to a walking pace kicked the rudder over to turn around and go find her man.

She saw him instantly. She always did. He was standing next to a brand shiny new pickup truck parked next to 78 Zulu. It said something of her besotted state that she didn't spare a glance for the Super Cub.

She couldn't just see Liam's smile from a thousand feet away, she could feel it. She always could. She made her way sedately to the tie-down and swung the tail around. She shut off the engine and the prop slowed and stopped. He caught the door in his hand as she opened it. "Hey."

She returned his smile with one of her own that seemed to light her face from within. Did he look like that when he looked at her? He pulled her down from the aircraft and onto the tarmac and at long, long last into his arms.

"Hey backatcha," she said, sounding breathless, her face turned up to his.

He looked at her for a long moment, his hands on her waist, her full, lush body firm against his, his own body already reacting because 'twas ever thus. "I missed you."

Her eyes roamed over him, hungry for every detail. The thick brown hair that gleamed with reddish lights fell over eyes so dark a blue they were like the sea at twilight. His nose was arrogant, his chin obstinate, his carriage commanding. He was tall and broad-shouldered and long-legged and drew the world's attention just by moving through it.

And he was smart, and funny, and kind. He was her lover and her best friend and her warm oasis in the indifferent desert that would be life without him. She could see his pulse beating in his throat and touched her fingers to it. "'I am to see to it that I do not lose you.'"

"What?" he said, deafened by the look in her eyes.

"Nothing. Just me channeling my inner Whitman. I missed you, too, Liam. Every day." She stood on her tiptoes, deliberately rubbing her body against his, and murmured against his mouth, "And every night."

With a will of their own his hands slid down over her ass and pulled her in tight against him and he forgot the world until someone gave a loud wolf whistle and someone else yelled, "Get a room!"

He pulled back to see that she was flushed and laughing. Neither of them cared enough to look around to see who was making fun of them. "Let's go home," he said.

"Does it have a bed?"

"Clean sheets and everything."

She stood on tiptoe and nipped at his bottom lip. "Take me there."

Six

Tuesday, September 3

HE WOKE EARLY AS HE ALMOST ALWAYS did, no matter how active the day—or night—before had been. In spite of the unfamiliar surroundings he knew immediately where he was and who was sleeping next to him. He turned to look at her, a graceful sprawl of woman, face down, a tumble of bronze hair, brown eyes closed. One arm tucked beneath her pillow revealed a plump curve of breast, right knee raised—he couldn't help himself and he didn't even try, raising his head to look at the dark mystery that upraised knee revealed. He did more than look. He positively gloated over all of the richness that was his to rediscover, exploit, debauch. He rolled up on his elbow to place a soft kiss at the base of her spine and was rewarded with a long, sensuous moan. He was already hard but that sound, man. Everything stood even more to attention.

"I can't," she said, voice muffled. "I'm dead. I am officially dead." She glared at him through her hair. "Killed dead by you, specifically."

"Uh-huh," he said, and knelt behind her, lifting her to her knees.

"Liam."

"Uh-huh." He slid one hand down her belly and between her legs.

"*Liam.*"

"I'm starving," she said.

"We did miss dinner," he said.

Explaining to each other why meant breakfast was even later. They ate it in bed. "Is Barton going to be pissed because you weren't in the office by eight?"

He licked the marmalade from her fingers. "I'm not officially on duty until Monday." He kissed her, enjoying the flavors of butter and orange and toast. And Wy. She was glowing. He didn't doubt that he was, too, and wouldn't have had a problem exhibiting that glow before anyone passing by. Preferably with his clothes on, but still.

"Yeah, but I know you. And I wish I didn't know him."

"What about you? What are your plans for the day?"

"I could just stay in bed. God knows I've earned it."

He laughed down deep in his throat.

She kissed him, stopping the laugh. He was perfectly

willing to shove the plates to the floor and push her back down on the sheets. It was a good look on her.

She laughed and slipped away from him. "My plans are to do form, shower, get dressed, and explore this new place you've dragged me to."

He caught her hand. "Dragged?"

Her expression softened. She leaned down to kiss him. "Joke. Not a very good one, evidently."

He was still wary. "Sure?"

She nuzzled his nose. "Too much bad history in Newenham. I was glad to leave it in the rear view. Pretty sure Tim felt the same."

There was more to it than that and they both knew it, but she wanted him to let it go, so he did. "You picking up your new car today?"

"It's twelve years old with 103,000 miles on it. Not exactly new."

"What did the shop say?"

"The guy said everything under the hood is good to go. Says there's a few parking lot dings and a chip in the windshield, but that's all cosmetic." She shrugged. "And, you know. It's a Subaru. It'll go until it drops."

"About every third car I've seen on the road here is a Subaru," he said. "Usually a Forester."

"It is the state car."

"True."

They did form together on the deck, Liam watching her for cues because she'd been at it a lot longer than he had.

They went through the thirty-two movements three times and as they straightened into Conclusion a bird called from the stretch of yard in front of them. Liam lost concentration and with it his balance. He put out a quick foot before he fell on his face and looked toward the call. Two sandhill cranes were stalking around like they owned the place. With their long legs and necks they looked like ungainly relics of the Jurassic Age. Which they were, as were all birds. But they weren't ravens, so there was that.

They admired their new view over a second cup of coffee. The house was one story, a rectangle thirty feet wide by fifty feet long. The long side stood twenty feet back from the edge of the tall bluff that overlooked all of Blewestown, the Bay, the glaciers, and the Kenai Mountains. On a clear day if they looked right they could probably see Kodiak.

Inside the house was an open floor plan, a large central room including kitchen, dining and living room. The master suite was on the left and two more bedrooms with a bathroom between were on the right. An arctic entryway faced the driveway with a guest bath just inside the door. A wooden deck ran the length of the house on the bluff side. The floors were wood laminate over radiant heat and the ceilings were vaulted. Wy got out her phone and pulled up the calculator app. "This house is almost exactly four times as big as my house in Newenham."

"It is a little palatial," Liam said, thinking about all the places he'd lived in Newenham. He'd slept in his office for way too long, moved from there to a boat in the small boat harbor that was literally sinking out from under him, and from there to a Jayco pop-up camper in Wy's driveway. Wy finally showed mercy and let him move in, and while her bed was only full size she was in it so no complaints. Here the bed was a California king, and also had Wy in it. He hoped he wasn't looking too smug. He was certainly feeling it.

"Not palatial. Just roomier. But homey. I like the living room furniture. Squashy." She kissed him. "It's not often that the reality is better than the pictures on Zillow."

"True." He savored the kiss. "You know, there's no real reason for us to leave the house at all today—"

His phone went off. The ringtone was Carly Rae Jepsen's "Everything He Needs." He looked up to see Wy making a kissy face at him. She must have changed it when he was in the shower.

He looked down at the screen and sighed. And of course it was Barton. Not a day went by that wasn't made better by a phone call from his boss.

Wy saw the name on Liam's phone and prudently moved herself out of the blast zone.

"Hello, John," he said, holding the phone at arm's length.

"WHERE THE FUCK ARE YOU, CAMPBELL!"

Even at arm's length Colonel John Dillinger Barton's bellow did tend to fill up a room. Liam worked his jaw back and forth to loosen up his eardrums. "I'm right here in Blewestown where you sent me, John."

"ABOUT FUCKING TIME!"

"Really didn't have to be here until next week," Liam said, with no hope of being heard.

There was no hope of a soft answer turning away wrath, either, as the director of the Alaska State Troopers carried on at full volume. "WE'VE GOT DEATHS BY METH INCREASING BY A THIRD EVERY FUCKING YEAR AND MOST OF THE HOMEGROWN IS COMING OUT OF THAT CESSPOOL THEY CALL THE LOWER KP! THE GOVERNOR IS ALL UP IN MY GRILL TELLING ME THE TROOPERS ARE FALLING DOWN ON THE GODDAMN JOB! GET WITH THE FUCKING PROGRAM, CAMPBELL! I WANT TO SEE NUMBERS CRASHING THE WAY THEY DID WHEN YOU AND CHOPIN WERE IN THE VALLEY!"

"Certainly, sir," he said.

Click. At least Barton wasn't slamming his cell phones down on his desk anymore. Probably because the department's bean counters got tired of paying for new ones.

Liam looked up to see Wy watching him with sympathy. "Yeah," he said. "Evidently I'm supposed to fix the meth problem in the entire state of Alaska all by myself."

"Well," she said, and grinned. "If anyone can do it…"

He flipped her off and she tossed her hair and gave him a smoldering look from beneath her eyelashes. "Anytime, anywhere, Campbell."

The local post was next to the local cop shop. He approved, as his post in Newenham had been isolated on a side road with nothing else around. Better for law enforcement to be smack in the middle of things. You had to be a neighbor before you could be a good neighbor. The Blewestown cop shop had brick walls and narrow windows and, unexpectedly, a colorful mural of sea otters frolicking in kelp on one side. His research had told him that it housed eight field officers, two administrative staff, and a chief with a no-bullshit reputation. Liam was looking forward to meeting him.

The trooper post was brand new and looked it, built on a template the Department of Public Safety had repeated all over the state. A square building sided with T-111 and roofed with asphalt shingles, it had a porch that faced the Bay, which surely the state had not paid for, as Alaska State Troopers were not encouraged to sit around outside admiring their own views. He was interested to see that there were solar panels on the roof, as well as on the roof of the cop shop. Jeff's comment about woke communities notwithstanding, if Blewestown was woke enough to support alternative energy he was all for it. Jeff and his wife had installed solar panels on their house and Jeff had shown Liam the electric bills. It was only one of the reasons they'd bought it, but it was definitely one of the reasons they could afford it.

The yard was a mess, a stretch of broken ground infested with dandelions and devil's club, with a few construction bricks, half a sack of pea gravel, and some rebar for garden art. He parked in front and walked up to the door. Somewhat to his surprise, it wasn't locked, and he went in.

He wasn't expecting to find anyone there before him, either. His mistake. The front office of the post occupied half of the floor space of the building. On one side of the room was a coffee table and a couple of armchairs. A table holding a coffee setup sat in one corner.

On the other side of the room was a desk placed at an angle so that it was the first thing one saw walking in. At this desk sat a young woman, early twenties, with narrow, tilted brown eyes and long brown hair. At first glance she reminded him of someone, although he couldn't think who. "Hi," he said. "I'm Liam Campbell."

Her spine visibly stiffened. She rose immediately to her feet and extended her hand in a gesture reminiscent of snapping a salute. "Sergeant Campbell. It is very nice to meet you, sir. I'm Sally Petroff, your administrative aide."

"I didn't know I had an administrative aide, and it's Liam," he said, shaking her hand. Her grip was firm but didn't linger. "Who hired you?"

"I interviewed for the job with Colonel Barton, sir."

The "sir" indicated that addressing him as Liam would be a work in progress. Okay then, tit for tat. "It's nice to meet you, too, Ms. Petroff. What's your background?"

"I was born in Kapilat across the bay. I have an AAS in Business Management from Charter College in Anchorage, and I spent a year working under Audrey Pratt in Colonel Barton's office, also in Anchorage. I'm fluent in APSIN,

ARMS, IRIS, ALDER, and OARS, and I can write dispatches upon request."

If she had survived training by Audrey Pratt, a martinet on the order of George S. Patton, she had smarts and stamina. He was mildly encouraged. "You're a local," he said. "Which means you know everybody. That will come in handy, since I'm not and I don't know anyone."

"Yes, sir."

"Relax, Ms. Petroff. You already got the job." She did not visibly relax, and he sighed inwardly. On top of everything else he had to break in a new employee, and he hated supervising. "Do I have an office?"

"You do, sir. Please follow me." A door in the back wall led to a small hallway with four doors off it, two on one side, two on the other, and a fifth with a screened window through which he could see a corner of the cop shop. "Those two are interview rooms, that's the bathroom, and that is the evidence room."

"I noticed the bank vault-worthy lock. You have the code?"

"I do. Here is your office." She opened the door and stood back. The room was just big enough to include a desk and a chair and two upright chairs across from it. There was a window in back of the desk, and that concluded the tour.

"Thank you," Liam said. He perched one hip on a corner of the desk and folded his arms. The more he looked at her, the more she reminded him of someone but he couldn't nail it down. "What is your job description, Ms. Petroff?"

She swallowed and, he could tell, immediately regretted

this betrayal of nerves. "All dispatches go through Soldotna, but I field any local calls. I keep your paperwork in order—Ms. Pratt was emphatic on the subject of tracking your overtime—and I liaise with Chief Armstrong's admin to ensure that all areas of our detachment are covered. You will have noticed the post has no holding cell."

Sidney Armstrong was Blewestown's police chief. "I have."

"Since this post was built simultaneously with Blewestown's new police headquarters, it was thought that as a cost-saving measure that this post could utilize their cells for any detainees we might have."

Before Liam could ask what other cost-saving measures there had been because bitter experience had taught him that there were always more, invariably to the detriment of whatever his mission was wherever he had been posted, they both heard the outer door open.

A woman was waiting for them in the front office. Medium height, medium though very curvy weight, blonde/green. "Shoot me now," Liam said.

"Sir?"

"Hey, Liam," the blonde said affably. "How you been?"

"Ms. Petroff?"

"Sir?"

"Does part of your job description include liaising with the press?"

"Sir, I interned four weeks with public relations, during which I wrote releases, fielded inquiries, and briefed three times."

"Excellent. Handle this, please?" Liam returned to his office and shut the door firmly behind him.

It opened as he was sitting down at his desk. "Nice try, Liam," the blonde said no less affably than before. "Don't blame the kid, she tried her best."

From behind her Petroff peered with a worried expression. "Sir, I'm sorry, but she just wouldn't—"

He waved her off. "Don't worry about it, Ms. Petroff. Carry on."

She did her best not to look too relieved.

"Don't worry, kid," Jo said. "This guy's a magnet for action. You'll be seeing a lot of me."

The door shut softly and Jo sat down across from Liam. They contemplated each other for a moment.

Jo Dunaway was a reporter for the *Anchorage News* and, for Liam's sins, his wife's college roommate at the University of Alaska and lifelong best friend. She was a very good reporter and an even better friend, and she enjoyed giving him wedgies in both of those roles. Payback was a way of life for Jo, and he was pretty sure she wasn't close to being done with paying him back for the heartache he had caused Wy in the early stage of their relationship. He didn't whine about it because he felt he deserved all the grief she handed out, and he never, ever made the mistake of complaining about Jo to Wy as Liam liked his head right where it was, thanks. He had to put up with Jo personally, so he did. He had to put up with her professionally, too, but he was a lot less sanguine about that.

"Little bit wired," Jo said.

"What?"

She hooked a thumb over her shoulder in the general direction of the front office. "Your sidekick."

"Oh." He couldn't deny it, so he said, "You have to know Wy's already here."

She nodded. "We texted."

"So. You're checking out my new post instead of our new house, because…?"

"Mostly I'm down here for a story."

"Swell. Can I call Wy for you?"

"We're meeting for lunch out on the Spit. What's hopping at your new post, Sergeant?"

"I'm not even officially here until next Monday."

"Barton cracking the whip?"

He looked at her and she laughed. "Yeah. That would have been way too easy." She stood up. "See you later."

"Why?"

"Didn't Wy tell you? I'm your first houseguest." And she was gone.

Great. Although he supposed he should be grateful Jo hadn't shown up yesterday. Possibly indicative of some small smidgeon of tact on her part.

He thought about it. Nah.

There was a tap at the door and he looked up to see Ms. Petroff standing in the doorway. "Who was that, sir?"

"That, Ms. Petroff, was an example of the species known as *Homo americanus diurnaria*." She looked confused, as well she might, and he relented. "She's a reporter for the *Anchorage News*. Jo Dunaway."

"Dunaway?" Her brow smoothed. "I've seen her byline. She wrote about Gheen."

"She did."

"There was another trooper—"

"Prince."

"Is she still in Newenham, sir?"

"No. So far as I know she's in Florida." Because she had eloped with Liam's father, that incorrigible womanizer otherwise known as Colonel Charles Bradley Campbell. Might be Brigadier General or Major General or even Lieutenant General by now. Probably never General, though, for which Liam sent up his heartfelt thanks to the United States Air Force. As a voter he thought his tax dollars could be better spent.

All of which Jo Dunaway knew full well, and with which information she used to needle him.

Ms. Petroff came all the way into the room. "Can I get you anything, sir?"

At least she wasn't going to dig around for the details of the Gheen murders as so many did when they found out he'd been the investigating officer. He nodded at the screen of the desktop computer. "Can you set this up so it answers to my password?"

"Of course, sir." He traded places with her and she busied herself at his keyboard. "There you are. Enter your password, confirm it, and you're good to go."

"Thank you, Ms. Petroff." He sat down again. She picked up his phone and handed it to him. "Please enter your passcode, sir?"

"Certainly." He did and handed the phone back.

She tapped away industriously and set it back down on the desk. "'Post' rings the landline on my desk. 'SP' is my cell number."

"Thank you," he said again, and studied her for a moment. She was of medium height but her erect posture made her seem taller. She was dressed in a neat two-piece pantsuit in dark blue with a white button-down underneath. She wore small silver hoops in her ears, no watch, no rings. Her nails were cut straight across and unpolished. She was very nearly a case study in professional anonymity. "You studied in Anchorage, you say?"

"Yes, sir."

"And then worked at HQ for a year."

"Yes, sir."

"When did you move back down to the Bay?"

"A month ago. When they finished the post."

"Have you found a place to live?"

"Yes, sir. A mother-in-law apartment over a garage. It's only a studio but very comfortable."

"Your landlord okay?"

"Yes, sir. It's my uncle's wife's sister and her husband. They fish commercially during the summer and grow coffee in Hawaii in the winter."

"Nice." He looked up. "Is there anything in particular

you'd like to draw my attention to, Ms. Petroff? Since you got here before me and have had time to settle in."

She hesitated, and he wondered if her advice had never before been solicited by a trooper. If her time on the job had been spent only at HQ, she would have seen more of politics than of policing, so perhaps not a surprise. "If you read through the last month's dispatches for this detachment, sir, it will do much to bring you up to speed. I..."

"Yes?" he said encouragingly.

"I believe Chief Armstrong would welcome an introduction, sir."

He nodded. "Anything else?"

"There's a local paper, sir, a weekly. It has a section called Cops and Courts. It would also help bring you up to speed."

That's right, they had an actual judge here in Blewestown; an actual judge in an actual courtroom in an actual courthouse. With jury trials. Which meant juries. God. "Should I introduce myself to the local judge as well?"

She nodded. "Yes, sir. I doubt that either of you want to meet for the first time in court."

He'd rather never meet another judge again as long as he lived. He wanted Bill back. Magistrate Bill Billington had taken no prisoners. She'd been a damn fine bartender, too. "No, probably not." He looked at the screen. "Why don't you call Chief Armstrong and ask him if he's free for lunch? Tell him to pick the restaurant."

"Very good, sir." She turned to leave.

"Ms. Petroff?" She looked over her shoulder. "Were either of your parents in the military?"

"No, sir?"

"Just a passing thought." He waved her away and clicked on the dispatch icon she had so helpfully and efficiently set up on his desktop, and plunged into the minutiae of a state trooper's life on the road system.

The phone on his desk beeped. "Yes?"

"Chief Armstrong says to meet him at noon at the Compass Rose Diner."

"Thank you, Ms. Petroff."

"And Judge DeWinter says she is free at three, if you'd care to meet her in her office then. She says please will you bring the coffee."

"I trust you know how she likes it, Ms. Petroff? And where to buy it?"

"Of course, sir."

"Then please tell the judge I'll see her then, and thank you again."

"You're welcome, sir."

Liam grinned at the door. For once in his life and, Liam was certain, entirely without intending to do so, it looked like Barton had done Liam a honking big favor.

Seven

Tuesday, September 3

HE RETURNED FROM LUNCH IN A thoughtful mood and sat in his truck outside the post for a few moments, reviewing the meeting just past. The Blewestown chief was in his mid to late fifties, bulky but not fat, head shaved, dark blue uniform all present and correct. He greeted the waitstaff by name; they in turn called him "Chief" or "Chief Armstrong" and were polite but not friendly.

To Liam, the chief was polite but not genial. When asked, he revealed that he'd lived in Blewestown all his life bar four years in the Marines. He revealed that he was still in the reserves and had seen time in the Sandbox, not a full tour, no, but active service. His parents had been commercial fishermen and he had been a drifter himself and fished across the Bay when his off time coincided with an opener. He was divorced with two children, both out of college, one an LPN at the local hospital, the other a biologist with the Alaska Department of Fish and Game in Anchorage.

"You're out of uniform," he said before Liam's butt had even hit the seat of his chair.

"It's being shipped," Liam said, and tried not to feel annoyed.

Armstrong answered Liam's questions directly, usually in simple declarative sentences. He didn't ask the same questions of Liam. Either he didn't care or he already knew, probably the latter. Liam was just a tad notorious in Alaska law enforcement, but Armstrong made only one remark that acknowledged that. "I followed the Gheen case."

Liam waited.

"I'm acquainted with Nina Stewart's family."

It took Liam a moment to remember. Nina Stewart had been Rebecca Hanover's staunch best friend. "I remember her on the news."

"Yeah, you don't fuck with Nina." Without changing expression or added emphasis, Armstrong said, "You should have killed the son of a bitch."

Liam swallowed the rage that rose every time someone said that to him. Many had. "I'm a state trooper, not an executioner."

The air cooled even further. Lunch arrived—okay burgers and soggy fries—and they ate without commentary. Afterward, Armstrong worked a toothpick around his teeth and said, "We haven't had a trooper assigned here for decades.

Usually your people are dispatched out of Soldotna. If we need them."

The implication being they didn't. Liam had wondered if he was about to be handed his hat and shown the door, metaphorically at least, and waited warily. Usually local law enforcement in Alaska was ecstatic for any kind of help, but Blewestown was on the road system and one of the state's larger communities, which bred a larger and more autonomous police department, mostly because it was easier to get help. It took something extra to live and work in the Bush; it took nothing extra to live and work on the road system. "I'm aware," he said.

The chief nodded. "Our area of responsibility only extends to the city limits. You, on the other hand, are responsible for everything that happens on the other side of those limits."

"Well." Liam tried a smile. "Not everything, I hope."

The chief did not smile back. "There are three Old Believer villages. They're pretty self-sufficient. They almost never call in. But there are an awful lot of people living out in the boonies who could use a little attention."

"I am aware," Liam said again.

"You'll need a four-wheeler."

"I'm told I'll have one, and a pickup with four-wheel drive."

The chief nodded. "A plane?"

"I don't fly."

"You'll need a pilot on call then." He jerked his head toward the view of the other side of the Bay, visible outside the window they were sitting next to. "Those folks generally keep themselves to themselves but they do need help on occasion."

Please god not too often, Liam thought.

"We should exchange phone numbers," the chief said. They did, and the chief picked up his hat.

Liam stood up with him. "Any ongoing cases of which I should be aware?"

The chief pulled on his cap. "Nothing to speak of."

Liam had followed him outside and watched him drive away.

Very odd, he thought now, tapping the steering wheel. He'd spent the morning looking at detachment dispatches, the files Barton had left him on a Google Drive file password-protected to the level of Defcon 5, and a map he could zoom into of the lower Kenai Peninsula. There were plenty of hot spots. If it had been him, he would have welcomed the help instead of actively distancing himself from it. "Was it something I said?" he said out loud.

Someone tapped at his window in time with his own fingers tapping on the steering wheel. He jumped, and turned his head.

Standing on the other side of the driver's door was the tiniest, oldest woman he'd ever seen in his life.

She was also naked.

She smiled at him, looking as if she might sprout wings at any moment (and certainly there was nothing in the way to preclude that) and said something he couldn't hear.

He rolled down the window. "I beg your pardon, ma'am?" he said, because it was the first thing that leaped to mind.

She smiled even more seraphically. "I knew just by looking at you that you would have good manners." She sniffed. "Or any manners at all. I wonder, could you give me a ride to Barney's? I'm going to be late for my first set, and Elmer gets so upset when that happens."

"Sure thing, ma'am." He groped for the jacket on the seat next to him.

He managed to talk her into his jacket, which reached her shins, and from there into the office. To oblige him she agreed to enthrone herself on one of the armchairs and made him promise again to find her a ride to Barney's in time for her set.

He turned and surprised Ms. Petroff with an almost human expression on her face. "Do you know her?" he said.

"Of course," she said, with what sounded like genuine affection. "That's Mrs. Karlsen."

Mrs. Karlsen heard her name and waved. "So nice to see you again, dear. How is your father these days?"

"He's fine, Mrs. Karlsen."

"Such a nice boy, Erik, so polite, and my goodness, so very handsome. You look very much like him, my dear."

Ms. Petroff seemed to stiffen. "I'll tell him you said so, Mrs. Karlsen."

"You do that, dear. And you'll see about my ride, won't you?"

"Of course, Mrs. Karlsen."

The old woman fussed with the lapel of Liam's jacket and looked at him with a frown. "Who are you again?"

"Sergeant Liam Campbell, Alaska State Troopers, Mrs. Karlsen."

"If you are in the troopers, Sergeant, why aren't you in uniform?"

"It's at the cleaners, ma'am." In a lower voice he said to Ms. Petroff, "Who is Mrs. Karlsen?"

"Sybilla Karlsen, sir," she said in an equally low voice. "She lives at Sunset Heights, up the hill and across Sourdough Street."

Liam could feel the beginnings of a slow burn, and reminded himself that he was a stranger in town. "And she made it this far without someone stopping to help her?"

"This would probably be the sixth or seventh time she's done this this summer, sir."

"What?" He cast an involuntary look over his shoulder and Mrs. Karlsen beamed at him.

"She's very wily, sir."

He drew in a deep breath and let it out. "What is done, generally, when she, ah, goes out for a stroll?"

"Generally, Sunset Heights is informed and they fetch her, sir."

Sunset Heights was informed and Mrs. Karlsen was duly fetched. Liam and Ms. Petroff stood on the porch, waving goodbye. "What was she talking about, late for her set at Barney's?"

"Barney's was a nightclub, sir, which Mrs. Karlsen owned and where she sang."

"In Blewestown?"

"Oh, no, in Anchorage. She was quite well known all over Alaska."

Liam regarded Ms. Petroff with fascination. "When was this, exactly?"

"In the sixties and seventies, I believe. During pipeline construction."

Liam had heard stories of the pipeline years and wondered what else went on inside Barney's besides singing. An unworthy thought. "How did she end up in Blewestown?"

"Her husband built the highway in 1960. They had a cabin here. When he died she sold her club in Anchorage and moved down."

"So she's alone now?"

"Her brother, Hilary, is still alive," she said with exactitude, by which inference Liam guessed Ms. Petroff thought Mrs. Karlsen might as well be alone in the world.

He moved the conversation to a more profitable topic. "I need a map, Ms. Petroff."

"Your laptop has access to Google Maps, sir. I installed it myself."

"And thank you for that, but I want a paper map of the entire lower Kenai Peninsula, one that includes the south side of the Bay as well. I want every little nook and cranny at as high a resolution as you can find. If it fit one entire wall of my office, I would not complain."

Ms. Petroff readjusted her ideas. "I'll see to it, sir."

He smiled at her. "I know you will." She was unaffected by either the smile or the approval. It wasn't the reaction he was accustomed to receiving from the fairer sex, and he might have pouted if he'd been that guy. He sternly repressed a grin. He looked at the clock on the wall and fortuitously, it was five minutes to three. "I'll go home after my audience with Her Honor."

"Yes, sir."

Eight

Tuesday, September 3

"**D**O YOU SEE HIM ANYWHERE?"

"Nah. Told you. The movie star had that big party last night and they all went."

"Erik, too?"

"Yeah."

"I'm still pissed they didn't let us go."

"R-rated."

"Like we couldn't dial up anything we wanted to online anyway." High-pitched middle school giggles. "Kinda cool, though."

"What?"

"Gabe inviting all the neighbors."

"Gabe?"

"He said to call him by his first name. That's kinda cool, too, right?"

"Eh. He just wants them all to help him get that ornament thing passed."

"Ornament? You mean like you put on the Christmas tree?"

Impatient with pedantry. "It's a word that sounds like that, I can't remember. He doesn't want the tourists knocking on his door."

"Who does?"

"At least they don't come down here. Mostly." A scrape of sneaker heel loosening a cascade of pebbles. "Watch out!"

"Here, grab on! Kyle, grab my hand!"

A yelp, a smack of butt, a crunch of grass, a tear of fabric, and a cross between a scream of panic and a whoop of delight, all ending in a soft thud.

"Kyle! Dude, are you okay? Kyle?" A clumsy, hurried scramble slightly more controlled than the first. Two feet solidly hit beach rock. "Kyle?"

"Get off! I'm fine. Except I think I got sand down my pants."

Another high-pitched giggle, this one tinged with relief. "Man, you should have seen yourself. You looked like you were coming down Mount Marathon on the Fourth of July." A pause. "You kinda look like you did, too. You're elbow's a mess."

"Shut up."

"Dude, what are you doing? Ew!"

"Shut up! I'm just trying to shake the sand out of my underwear."

"I sure hope none of those people out on boats have their binocs on you. Wow, that's like a sand wedgie in there."

"Shut up. Is anybody around?"

"I think we'd know by now."

"Shut up."

"You shut up. Want to look in the tent?"

"I didn't slide down that mountain just to poke around in the tide pools."

"It's not a mountain. Okay, then, come on."

Not-so-stealthy footsteps, a rasp of canvas.

"It's just a bunch of junk."

"I don't know. The arrowheads are kind of cool. We could make a bow and—"

"Come on, Kyle. Erik would kill us dead if he knew we'd been messing with his stuff."

"He should lock it up when he goes home, then."

"Come on, Kyle. Erik's a good guy."

"You just want him to teach you how to be a—a anus-ologist."

"It's archeologist and you know it."

"Hey, look, a cave! Grab that flashlight, Logan. Man, it's dark in here."

"Duh. It's a cave."

"How far back does it go?"

"I have a bad feeling about this, Kyle. We should go."

"Man, this goes back pretty far. I thought this side of the Bay was all sand."

"Silt. From the glaciers."

"Whatever. Hey, there's a little crack here. I think I can reach through it."

"Careful, there might be something waiting to munch you on the other side."

"Shut up. I think I can—"

"Kyle, wait, what are you doing?"

"Hand me the flashlight. Hey. I think there's another cave."

"Kyle, I don't think you should—"

"I think I can—"

"Where are you going? Kyle—"

A high, excited giggle. "Man, you think it's dark out there!" Scrabbling sounds. "Oh shit!" A trip, a startled cry, a thunk, some more swearing.

"Kyle! What happened? Are you okay?"

Kyle screamed.

Nine

Tuesday, September 3

"NICE PLACE."

"Nice, my ass, it's gorgeous."

Jo laughed. "You win, it's gorgeous. How big?"

"About fifteen hundred square feet, I think Liam said."

"Not necessarily a McMansion."

"Don't need one. Let's check out the garden." They went through the door that opened onto the deck and perambulated around the yard that stretched to the edge of the bluff. Someone had been ruthless in keeping the brush trimmed pretty close to the ground between the deck and the edge of the bluff, and Wy glanced back at the house. Of course, to protect the view.

The yard was edged with flowers, almost all of them bloomed out by now but there were a few Shasta daisies left. "I think these are mostly Alaska wildflowers," Wy said when they came to the end of the circuit. "Cranesbill, Arctic iris, sedum, starflowers. Is that a daylily?"

"Since when are you an authority on Alaska wildflowers?"

"I know a forget-me-not when I see one."

Jo came to a stop at the front of the yard and looked out at the view. The airport was front and center, with the Spit pushing out into the Bay in back of it. "What's the elevation here?"

"About a thousand feet, Liam said."

"Spring is gonna be late and winter will be early." Jo turned to survey the house and grounds. "How much land comes with the house?"

"Twenty acres, ten more or less on each side of the road."

Jo smiled. "Enough room to mow your own strip."

Wy smiled. "Liam said there was one put in by the original homesteader. It wasn't maintained and the fireweed overran it. We'll have to buy a mower or hire somebody with one."

Jo turned to face Wy directly. "What's next?"

Impossible to pretend to Jo. "I don't know, exactly."

Jo gestured at the airport and at the lake that hosted the seaplane base. "Plenty of flying available here, it looks like."

"There are already two air taxis and half a dozen flight-seeing operations in business on the Bay."

"Yes, and an FBO with a G-2 parked out in front of it. You built up a good business in Newenham, Wy. Had to hurt to leave it behind."

Wy shook her head once with a finality Jo had to recognize. "It was time to move on."

"The relatives in Icky getting to be too much of a pain?"

Wy shrugged.

Jo knew that obstinate look. "You're a little too young to retire."

"I imagine I'll pick up some jobs here and there while I figure out what I want to do with the rest of my life."

As if on cue, Wy's cell rang, and Jo laughed when she heard the ringtone.

Wy, a little flustered, turned her back. "Hey. We're both here at the house. You? Okay, that sounds good." She looked over her shoulder at Jo. "You, too." She hung up.

Jo, still laughing, said, "Your ringtone for Liam is 'I Want Your Sex'?"

"No," Wy said, pink staining her cheeks, "my ringtone for everyone is 'Sweet Child O' Mine' but Liam thinks it's funny to change my ringtone to whatever he wants when I'm not looking."

Jo's laughter faded and her voice was gentle when she spoke again. "You thinking of adopting again?"

"Because the last attempt went so well?"

"She had family."

"Yeah, and my relatives in Icky helped so much." Wy sighed. "I'm thirty-eight, Jo, and Liam says he doesn't care one way or the other."

Prudently, Jo kept her own counsel on the matter. With determined lightness she said, "And Tim could provide you with some grandchildren. I dropped into Seward on the way down, took him out for a burger. He looks good.

He coming down here when he's got his A and P license?"

"We'd like that, of course, but he'll need to go where the jobs are."

Jo hooked a thumb over her shoulder. "I'm seeing plenty of airplanes at the Blewestown airport."

"What about you?" Wy said. "You and Mason still making the beast with two backs?"

Jo grinned. "When we feel so moved."

Wy flung up a hand. "Spare me the details, please."

"You asked. How long can I stay?"

"Long as you want. Plenty of room."

Jo gave her the side-eye. "I expect Liam will be overjoyed to hear that."

"Liam has a bedroom door with a lock on it and me on the right side of the lock. Liam won't care."

Jo laughed out loud. "So that answers any questions I might have about how things are with you and Liam."

"I'm not flying today," Wy said. "Let's break open a bottle of wine."

⁂

The courthouse was a sprawling, one-floor building with gray siding and a lot of spruce trees crowding up like they wanted to personally hear testimony in all the cases. The grass beneath one of them rustled and he saw a pair of spruce grouse pecking busily away at the pine cones scattered on the ground. Not ravens, which was good.

Judge DeWinter was in her fifties, five-five, untidy blonde hair going to gray, brown eyes, and a chin like Ben Affleck before the beard. She produced a bottle of Glenlivet and motioned for him to bring two paper cups from the coffee setup on the credenza across the room. "Sit," she said, pouring.

He and Judge DeWinter were going to get along just fine. He traded her coffee for his Scotch. The smell of eighteen-year-old single malt hit his nostrils and he froze in place with the cup just inches from his lips. But not for long. "Thank you, Your Honor," he said with feeling.

"Long day?"

"Just getting used to the territory. And the help. Takes some concentration."

She cocked an eyebrow. "And you're in mufti."

"What does that even mean, Judge?"

"Means you're not in uniform, and so might not be experiencing that deference your office might otherwise expect."

"I've had some issues with my uniforms in the past." He looked down at his Pendleton shirt and jeans, worn at elbows and knees but otherwise clean and neat. "And I'm not officially on duty until next Monday." She snorted. "Ah," he said. "You know Colonel Barton then."

"We've met."

"In court?"

She toasted him and sipped. "Indeed."

A battle of the Titans, he thought. Or maybe just the immovable object meeting the irresistible force. Would have been nice to have had a front row seat to that. So long as he wasn't testifying.

"You were the trooper who found the wreck of the World War II plane."

"Not personally, no, but I investigated the cases that were associated with it."

"I'm an Alaska history buff," she said. "Bunch of planes lost in Alaska during that war."

"May be the first murder solved by global warming," he said. "If the weather hadn't warmed up to the point that that glacier melted to where the plane crashed into it, people would still be looking." He sipped again and let the Scotch sit for a moment on his tongue. "Are you aware of why I'm here?"

"I helped Barton build the files he gave you."

He sipped, waiting.

"I get tired of seeing the same faces up before me year after year." She drained her cup, refilled it, and held up the bottle. He shook his head and she recorked it and made it disappear. He mourned a little but then he had Glenmorangie at home. "And a lot of those people are becoming nuisances to their neighbors. I don't know what it is about meth cookers and junkyards, but as soon as one shows up the other follows."

She spoke with a certain bitterness and he hazarded a guess. "One of your own neighbors, perhaps?"

Her smile was as frosty as her name. "Perhaps."

"You live outside the city limits?"

Her expression didn't change but there was some feeling there he couldn't quite detect. "You've met Chief Armstrong then."

"We had lunch."

She evidently had no intention of bringing him into the loop at this early stage of their relationship. "In fact I do live outside the city limits."

Liam foresaw a cruise down the judge's street in his very near future, and made a mental note to have Ms. Petroff look up the judge's street address at her earliest convenience.

"I want probable cause every time, Sergeant Campbell." This was the judge speaking now, not the fellow drinker next to him at the bar, and his spine straightened. "No shortcuts or no warrants. Am I rightly understood?"

He very nearly saluted. "You are, ma'am."

"I don't give a damn how badly you or I want them, I don't even care how guilty they are, they cross the line first. You have reasonable grounds as defined by statute and precedent you can wake me up at three a.m. if you want." She reflected. "My husband may have an issue with that but that's his problem." She bent a stern glare on him. "And no rough stuff. I mean none."

Liam tried not to take offense, but his voice hardened nonetheless. "I don't do rough stuff, Your Honor."

"Hold that thought. The academy should have given you all the de-escalation training you need and I know this because I consulted for the panel that wrote their standards. If I catch even a whiff of excessive force used on any defendant you bring before me I will shitcan your case on the spot and thereafter make it my mission in life to hound you out of the Alaska State Troopers and if necessary the state of Alaska itself. Are we clear?"

"Yes, ma'am," he said smartly.

"When was your last refresher?"

"Two years ago."

She grunted. "I recommend you immediately form working relationships with the homeless shelter, the women's shelter, the food bank, the public assistance office, and the community mental health center. You'll be able to hand off a lot of the situations that you encounter on your calls if you have all of them on speed dial. It would help if they knew who was calling."

Liam noticed she hadn't included the local PD and wondered why.

"What do you know about the community itself?"

He marshaled his thoughts. "Blewestown has some of the lowest per capita crime stats in the state. The economy runs mostly on summer tourism, but a lot of Alaskan gray hairs from Fairbanks and Anchorage are building vacation and retirement homes here, which might explain why there are two brewpubs, three coffee roasters and, for once in an Alaskan community, the bars outnumber the churches. And excellent Wi-Fi, too, which was a nice surprise."

"Newenham not so much?"

"One meg download speed."

"Not a streaming hotspot, then."

"It was faster to print out and mail a report than it was to try to upload it online."

She nodded. "What else?"

"There's still some commercial fishing, salmon, halibut, and cod, but they deliver to the only processor left on the Bay in Engaqutaq. There seems to be a thriving arts community with an accent on music, including two festivals, one in the spring and one in the fall. One high school, two middle schools, two grade schools. If you don't count the charter schools, which seem to pop up like mushrooms everywhere you look." He blessed Wy for having looked all this stuff up before they made the decision to move.

"And shrivel up again the moment they've managed to rake in as much federal funding as they can," she said, nodding.

"There's a homeless problem but then there's a homeless problem everywhere you look, in Alaska and Outside."

"And a drug trade, mostly homegrown meth, that is increasing by leaps and bounds. Barton's not wrong about that. Sometimes I think Walter White didn't die after all; he just moved north." She saw his blank expression and sighed. "Right, no streaming in Newenham. Well, Sergeant Campbell, my recommendation to you is that you spend the next few weeks driving around your new command." She hesitated and he tried to look mild and uninquiring because it was always after those kinds of pauses that the authority figures gave you the good stuff. "I would especially recommend that you familiarize yourself with just where the boundaries of city and state meet." She met his eyes steadily. "The local police chief can be touchy about jurisdiction."

"Can he," Liam said thoughtfully, and in an excess of diplomacy decided not to mention the mediocre burgers and even more lukewarm reception he'd received at lunch.

She tossed her empty cup in the trash can, where it banked off the rim and fell neatly inside. "You find a place to live yet?"

"My wife and I bought a house up on the bluff. Used to belong to Jeff Ninkasi."

She nodded. "Good people, Jeff, and he brews good beer. Nice house, too." She sat back. "Well, thanks for coming in, Sergeant, I appreciate the courtesy."

"Ms. Petroff informed me that I probably didn't want to meet you for the first time in court."

"Sally Petroff? She's working for you?"

"Colonel Barton hired her and had her in place before I got here."

"She good people, too, and she's local, which should help."

"What I thought." He stood up, holding his trooper ball cap by the bill. "I asked her if either of her parents had been in the military."

The judge laughed.

⸙

Liam pulled into the driveway of the house on the edge of the Blewestown bluff already with a sense of homecoming.

And then he walked in the front door and saw Jo. "Oh," he said.

"How was your day, dear?" she said, so sweetly that one could barely feel the acid drip-drip-dropping onto the skin. "Have a good time driving around in that penis extender of yours?"

He hooked a thumb over his shoulder in the general direction of the Jeep Cherokee Chief looming over the driveway. "You should talk."

Wy's laugh was husky and delicious as always, and for just a moment he was content just to look at her, smiling up at him from the couch, her bronze mane coming loose from its thick braid to form little curls around her face, her brown eyes warm and inviting, her cheeks a little flushed from the half-empty glass of red wine in her hand. If every day of his life ended with him walking in the door and seeing her like this he would die a happy man.

Jo looked from one to the other and rolled her eyes. "Young love. Gag me."

"We eating in or out tonight?" Liam said.

Wy finished off her glass and stood up. "In. I got a take-out lasagna and Jo tossed a salad."

Did you check it for wolfsbane? Liam wanted to say, but didn't.

"Look!" Jo said, pointing.

A moose cow and calf had wandered into the yard, stripping fireweed stalks of their flowers. They moseyed around the perimeter of the yard and vanished into the trees.

"It always amazes me how they disappear like that," Jo said.

"I know, right? They're so big."

Wy handed Liam a big wooden bowl full of green. "Table's set and the lasagna is ready to come out of the oven."

"Great, I'm starved. I had the world's most uninspired burger for lunch."

They sat down at the dining room table and dished out. "What brings you to Blewestown, Jo?" Liam said.

"I'm on vacation," Jo said blandly, and in spite of himself Liam laughed out loud.

Jo, amazingly, laughed, too. "Yeah, all right. I assume you saw the big rig parked up the Bay when you came into town."

"It was hard to miss," Liam said dryly.

"On lease to RPetCo. They want to do some exploratory drilling."

"In the actual Bay?"

She nodded. "There's oil and gas being produced in commercial quantities up and down the Inlet. Chungasqak Bay is the next geographical step, and it's a hell of a lot more accessible than, say, the Kamishak. Easier to supply, too, with Blewestown right here and on the road. They've got a deepwater dock, too."

"All the mod cons." The lasagna wasn't bad. He dished up a second slice. "I'd have to guess there are one or two people unhappy at the prospect."

Jo snorted. "Good guess. Most of the tourism businesses in town and all the fishermen, just for starters. The Chamber of Commerce, run by a guy named Donohoe, is giddy at the prospect of overseeing the next Prudhoe Bay, but he has to keep it on the down low as half of the chamber members are fishermen and they all talk like they're watching *Deepwater Horizon* on repeat. About a dozen small cruise ships a year dock here and their industry rep doesn't sound thrilled, either, but is otherwise making no move."

"Where is the local Native association on the issue?"

"There are a bunch of them, about one per community. One, the Kapilat Native Association, invested in bandwidth back in the day so they've got a lot of money and therefore the loudest voice. Generally speaking the others follow their lead. They haven't stated their position on oil exploration and development on the Bay, but I'm trying to get an interview with their chief, Alexei Petroff. So far I've only talked with him on the phone. He sounds pretty savvy but he doesn't want to go on the record unless it's face to face."

Wise man, Liam thought. Petroff would get the biggest bang for his association's buck by announcing their stand in the state's paper of record. He wondered if Petroff was any relation to She Who Must Be Obeyed in his front office.

"Lately, an archeologist has been making a fuss about the oil companies putting the human history of the Bay at risk."

Liam perked up. "That be Erik Berglund?"

"You've met him?"

Liam nodded. "Yesterday, at the brewpub. He invited me up to take a look at his dig so I did."

"What's he like?"

"Six-two, blond, blue, fortyish. The dig's a tiny little thing, more of a cave, and he hasn't found much. He's got a theory about a traditional trail that sounds pretty interesting, though."

"Fanatic?"

Liam reflected. "I don't think so. Just a true believer. I liked him. You don't find that many people that excited about their work." He looked at Jo. "So he's against the drilling?"

She nodded. "RPetCo has their own pet archeologist, a guy who's been pretty much a paid shill for resource extraction companies in Alaska for decades. No resource extraction company wants to be hindered by a lot of unnecessary restrictions that will only delay production."

"What would the shareholders say," Wy said.

"May you live in interesting times," Liam said.

"Yes, and now here comes Alaska state trooper Sergeant Liam Campbell into the mix. Why are you here, Liam?"

Liam exchanged a fleeting look with Wy and said, "Barton wanted me here to give the new post a push."

"Uh-huh."

"I told you, Jo," Wy said sternly. "It was time to leave Newenham."

It didn't satisfy the Torquemada wannabe but it did shut her up, and Liam tried not to look too grateful.

They finished dinner and Liam cleaned up and started the dishwasher. It ran at a low murmur. So far everything in this house was as advertised, and Liam decided it was high time he developed a palate for beer. For the moment he poured himself a finger of Glenmorangie and joined the women in the living room, where Wy had a fire going in the wood stove.

The glass was an inch away from his lips when his phone sang out with the first bars of "Need You Tonight." He gave Wy a look. "Seriously, Wy? A boy band?"

He kept the grin off his face until he was out on the deck, facing away from the two women in the living room giggling like teenagers. "Liam Campbell."

"Hey, Liam, it's Gabe McGuire." There was a sigh. "I know it's late and I apologize, but I think I'd be in trouble if I waited until morning to call this in."

"Did you try the local cops?" That might have come out a little more crankily than he'd meant it to.

"I'm outside the city limits. They won't respond if I'm not paying property taxes in Blewestown."

A twittering sound filled the air and he looked up to see a flock of cedar waxwings swirl past. There were several mountain ash in the yard and they assembled into a fluttering, quarreling mess to fight over the berries.

"Liam?"

Liam's turn to sigh. "Tell me what's up and I'll decide if I want to wait until morning."

Ten

Tuesday, September 3

GABE MCGUIRE DIDN'T LOOK ANY HAPPIER to be answering his door than Liam was to be knocking on it. The same could not be said of the two ten-year-olds in the living room. They sported one parent each, a mom and a pop. The kids looked wide awake and wired for sound. Their 'rents each held a phone like they had their attorneys on speed dial.

The house looked less massive from the inside than the roof had indicated from the road. The main feature was floor-to-ceiling windows that went from wall to wall, cathedral ceilings over a hardwood floor, and a lot of mix and match furniture that had only the maximum amount of stuffing in common, including the dining table, if wood could be stuffed. There wasn't a screen in sight except for the phones everyone was holding, which Liam found mildly surprising. "Explain to me, please, preferably in words of one syllable, why I am here," he said.

McGuire looked over his shoulder. "Who's that?"

"This is Jo Dunaway, with the *Anchorage News*. She's a friend of the family." It had been impossible to keep her out of the pickup, and Wy had been no help.

"A cop and a reporter," McGuire said. "If this isn't just the cherry on my day. Could you wait right here while I leg it out the back door?"

"You called me," Liam said. "I can go home any time."

McGuire's shoulders raised on a sigh. "Ms. Dunaway."

"Mr. McGuire."

"This isn't a story."

Jo gave him her best T-rex impersonation. "I'm just here with friends."

When she moved McGuire saw Wy and brightened. "Ah, you brought the hot pilot, too. You're forgiven. Good to see you again, Ms. Chouinard." He smiled at Wy and Wy smiled right back.

McGuire was trying to be polite and Liam wasn't so far gone he didn't recognize it but he still bristled. Nobody flirted with Wy but him. He didn't need Jo Dunaway grinning like the Cheshire Cat all over her face, either.

"Can I get you something to drink?"

Liam tried not to glare. "You gave me to understand that this wasn't a social call."

"It isn't."

"So? I'm here because…?"

"Well, you, specifically, are here because the Blewestown PD say they won't respond to anything outside of the city limits. They say that's for the troopers to handle. A direct quote from whoever answered the phone and took down my name and in particular my address."

Liam thought of Chief Armstrong's polite but obdurate attitude over lunch earlier that day. "Okay. Fine. What requires any law enforcement presence outside the city limits at ten at night?"

McGuire looked across the room. "All yours, Kyle."

Upon closer inspection, Kyle, the skinny kid with the bright gray eyes and dark hair, looked a little the worse for wear. His hair stuck up in sweaty wads and the sides of his face were scratched and oddly shiny. His left ear might be a little lopsided, too, and the collar of his T-shirt was irregularly stained a dark brown, as if he'd been bleeding on it and the blood had dried there. He looked around at his audience, clearly enjoying the attention, and puffed out his insubstantial chest. "I found a body!"

Into the resulting dead silence that followed, during which Liam felt rather than saw Jo Dunaway go on red alert, the second kid, slightly less skinny but considerably wider of eye and with hair in infinitely better shape said, "I told you I had a bad feeling about this."

"And you are?" Liam said.

"Logan," McGuire said. "That's Logan. And that's Logan's mom, Cynthia Reese, and that's Kyle's dad, Greg Kinnison."

Liam nodded at both of them. "Nice to meet you. Liam

Campbell, Alaska State Troopers." He looked back at Kyle. "What do you mean, you found a body?"

The stern note in his voice caused Kyle's grin to fade a little. "I mean we found a body."

"You mean you found a body," Logan said, although it was more of a mutter.

Kyle gave him an impatient shove. "Shut up. And I can prove it."

"Dude, you're just going to freak them the hell out."

"Logan!" his mother said. "Language."

Kyle ignored them both and reached down to unbutton the pocket on the calf of his cargo pants, which also looked much the worse for wear. He produced a package wrapped clumsily in what looked like paper towels. He slid to his knees on the floor and with a due sense of ceremony folded back the towels to reveal what was within. Cynthia looked ill and averted her eyes. Greg folded his arms and tried to out-manly the trooper and the movie star.

Liam heard Wy draw in a quick breath and he said to Jo in a low voice, "Not a word. Not yet."

Kyle, a little apologetically, said, "It kind of fell apart when I grabbed it."

It was a collection of small bones. Finger bones, if Liam was not mistaken, and he had the sinking feeling that he wasn't. "You said a body, Kyle."

"The rest of it is still back there, sir. This was all I could reach before they pulled me out."

"Pulled you out of where?"

"Out of the cave."

Liam looked at Gabe.

"Erik's dig."

Liam sat down. "Maybe you should start at the beginning."

"Yes, please," Jo said, and ignored the look of death Liam sent her.

"You sure I can't get you something to drink?" Gabe said.

It transpired that the boys had taken advantage of Erik's absence to explore Erik's dig and the cave behind it. During said exploration, they had discovered a crack at the back of said cave. Kyle found that his arm fit in the crack, which inspired him to see if his head could fit in it, too. At which point he became stuck. After futile efforts to extract him that resulted in the marks of mauling on display on Kyle's face, Logan went for help.

"Why you?" Liam said.

"Mine's the closest house."

McGuire had sent Logan to alert the parents—the Kinnisons and the Reeses lived off the same driveway nearer to East Bay Road—and had gone down to the cave to see what he could do. "I'll give you this, dude, when you get stuck into something you really commit."

Kyle looked hugely delighted to be called "dude" by Gabe McGuire. Logan scowled at his shoes.

Gabe looked at Liam. "So then I thought maybe if I got some grease or something, that might work him loose, so I brought down a bottle of olive oil."

No wonder Kyle's hair looked so weird.

Kyle grinned and Gabe laughed. "I poured the whole thing over as much of his head as the neck of the bottle would reach and I told him to rub it in. It worked."

"Cool, huh?" Kyle said proudly. Logan rolled his eyes.

"About which time," Gabe said, "Logan showed back up with Cynthia and Greg in tow. And then we called you."

"Okay," Liam said, "am I to understand that these bones came from the other side of the crack?"

"Yep." Kyle nodded vigorously. "And that's not all. When Gabe went back for the oil I felt around for the flashlight I'd dropped when I got stuck and shined it around. And—" building for a big finish "—that's when I saw it!"

"Saw—"

Kyle pointed at the bones. "The rest of the body! The whole skeleton! It's kind of crumpled up but you can tell right away what it is! There's a spine, and legs and a skull and everything!" He paused, and then, clearly unhappy at the response to this earthshaking announcement, added, "The whole thing is still there!"

"You want to go take a look?" Gabe said.

Liam glanced up at the windows, behind which the sun had without question set. He was not attempting that death-defying trail in the dark. "Tomorrow, maybe. Have you talked to Erik?"

"I called him but he didn't pick up. Let me try again." Gabe picked up his phone, called up a number, and held the phone to his ear. After a minute or so he shook his head. "Still not picking up. Probably keeping company somewhere.

Guy gets more action than any other ten men on the Bay, including me."

Cynthia cleared her throat meaningfully, and Gabe didn't quite blush.

Wy, speaking and possibly moving for the first time since coming into the house, smiled impartially at Cynthia and Greg. "Isn't there school tomorrow?"

Greg said, "Yeah, Logan, time to head for the barn."

"Yes, Kyle, way past your bedtime," Cynthia said.

"C'mon, Mom—"

"And we're going to have a conversation about your choice of friends first thing tomorrow."

"What?" Greg said.

"It wasn't my fault!" Logan said. "It wasn't even my idea!"

"Let's go, Kyle." Cynthia bustled toward the door, outrage in the line of her spine.

Kyle looked at Greg. "She gets like this, Mr. Kinnison. Don't worry about it, Dad'll calm her down." He looked at Liam. "Can I keep the bones?"

"Nope," Liam said.

"Didn't think so," Kyle said regretfully, "but it was worth the ask." He grinned at Logan and extended a fist. Logan bumped it with his own. "Later, dude."

"Later."

The Kinnisons *père et fils* followed Kyle out the door.

"Erik never said anything about a cave behind a cave when he was showing me around," Liam said.

"Never did to me, either."

"Could he have not known it was there?"

Gabe gave him a look. "Wait till you see the opening. It's barely worthy of being called a crack."

"Yeah, but he's an archeologist. Don't they, like, survey everything and measure it twice?"

"Everything he found he found on that shelf in the outer cave, so far as I know," Gabe said. "And he only found it a couple of weeks ago. Maybe he hasn't gotten around to it yet." He look at Liam, curious.

"What?"

"You don't seem too excited at the prospect of finding a human skeleton on your watch."

Liam shrugged and stood up. "For one thing, it might not be human." He walked over to the pitiful little pile of bones and folded them back up into the towel. "Before I try to fit through a crack Kyle couldn't get his head through, I'd like to find out if that really is what we have here."

McGuire's eyebrows went up. "You think it isn't?"

"Absolutely no doubt Kyle believes it is," Liam said. He raised the package. "The bones definitely look like disconnected phalanges to me, and I've seen a few in my time."

"But?"

"But animal bones have been mistaken for human bones many a time, especially bear bones and especially in Alaska."

"Who can say for sure?"

"I'm guessing Erik Berglund can. I'll give him a call in

the morning. If he still doesn't answer, I'll ask Ms. Petroff to find someone."

"Who?"

"Trust me, she'll know."

Eleven

Wednesday, September 4

LIAM WOKE UP IN HIS OWN BED WITH HIS arms wrapped around his own wife for the second glorious morning in a row. Her back was warm against his chest, her breast rose and fell against his arm, her curls tickled his nose, the skin of her neck was soft against his lips. He was in that moment utterly, completely content.

And then his phone rang. Still the boy band but they both jumped anyway. "If it's Barton tell him I'm coming for him," Wy mumbled into her pillow. "With extreme prejudice."

He groped for his cell and squinted at the screen. It was Barton. It was also six a.m. He turned the phone off and tossed it down somewhere. He might have heard it hit the floor and since it was the property of the state of Alaska he should have been more concerned, but there was nothing more important in his life than curling his body around Wy's and luxuriating in this moment.

Wy yawned. "What time is it?"

"Six a.m."

"Must have been important."

"Not necessarily. And I don't care."

He heard the smile in her voice. "If you're about to get fired I'd better step up the effort to find a new job."

"Take your time. No one else wanted this post, and I'm starting to figure out why."

She rolled onto her back and stretched. "Stand by one." She visited the bathroom and he enjoyed the view afforded by both trips. She snuggled in beneath the covers, tucking her head beneath his chin. He could feel her breath on his collarbone when she spoke. "Tell me."

"Well, for starters, there's Ms. Petroff, my administrative aide. Hired by Barton and in the office long before I got here. She's from across the Bay and seems to know the Bay chapter and verse. I hope I am speaking metaphorically there but I'm not quite sure. She is almost terrifyingly efficient."

"And local, so she'll know everyone."

"Yes, including one Mrs. Karlsen, a self-described torch singer, who showed up at the post looking for a lift to the bar she sings at."

Wy yawned and snuggled closer. "A torch singer."

"Indeed. I should probably add that she is retired and that the bar she sang at closed thirty years ago. Also, there seems to be some indication that Sybilla sang in the nude, because she was certainly prepared to go to work that way."

There was a momentary silence, and Liam felt her go very still. "I beg your pardon?"

He grinned into her hair. "Sybilla is in her eighties and lives at Sunset Heights, which Ms. Petroff gives me to understand is assisted living. She says it isn't Sybilla's first escape attempt."

"You might have to pay them a call to discuss their security measures."

"And I would, except Sunset Heights is within the Blewestown city limits, and Chief Armstrong, with whom I had lunch, has given me to understand that my writ does not carry within those limits. I am to confine myself to infractions committed within the jurisdiction of the state."

She did raise her head at that, and he smoothed back the tangle of curls. "You're kidding."

"Not in so many words, but that was the distinct impression I was given, and most deliberately so."

"Huh."

"Eloquently put. Further investigation is required, but for now I'm on my own. He volunteered no information, either, so I'll have to rely entirely on state records and whatever I can dredge out of the Soldotna post. I'm hoping they'll be a little friendlier."

"You'd think."

"And then I dropped in on the local judge, who offered me a shot of Glenlivet, so naturally I'm already inclined to think kindly of her, or I was until she told me I couldn't beat up anybody."

She wriggled up to put her head on the pillow next to his so she could see him. "You don't beat up people."

"What I told her."

"And her reply?"

"She asked me if I'd been through the course at the academy, and then wanted to know when I'd taken my last refresher."

"Insulting."

"A little," he said. "But only a little. Excessive force is not a joke and it's not the worst thing for a judge to be concerned about." He hesitated.

"What?"

"I don't know, I guess I—I'm wondering where that came from. If the judge was moved enough by the issue to warn me off before I even pulled someone over for a broken taillight..."

"You think the local LEOs trend that way?"

"I don't know. Maybe. I hope not." He shifted restlessly and changed the subject. "What's on your agenda for today?"

"Check on the aircraft. Maybe wander around the lake, poke my head into the air taxis and flightseeing companies."

"I saw what looked like an FBO north of the terminal."

"With a G-2 parked in front of it, yeah. I'm not looking for a job on the ground. Especially not one where I have to cater to people who have more money than sense who you just know are going to want to fly and shoot same day."

"You want something on the reg, or for hire."

"All I know for sure is I don't want to work with assholes."

He laughed. "Right there with you, babe." He kissed her. Things were just getting interesting when muffled sounds came from beyond the door. He groaned. "Jo's up. How long is she here for again?"

Her turn to grin. "You worried she might move in permanent?"

He rolled his eyes, but indeed it was not the least of his worries. Wy's parents were disengaged, almost asocial, and so not much present in their daughter's life, other than insisting that she get a college degree. So Wy had built her own family, beginning with Jo, her college roommate, and Jo's family, including a brother of whom Liam would rather not think.

"Dibs on the shower," Wy said. She got up and stretched while he admired the view again. "Agatha Christie said your house had to be big enough not to bump your bum on the furniture while you were cleaning. Even the bathrooms are roomy in this house." She grinned at him over her shoulder. "The beer business must be good."

"I think it is if you know what you're doing."

They presented themselves in the kitchen, cleaned and scrubbed and possibly a little too self-satisfied, because Jo rolled her eyes at first look. "Coffee's on." A ding. "And the monkey knuckles are ready to come out of the oven."

"Oh, boy." As one they rushed for the oven. The monkey knuckles, miniature tear-apart cinnamon rolls, were a rich, crusty, brown glistening with sugar and butter and smelled like heaven. "Yum."

They sat down at the dining room table and tried not to make pigs of themselves.

"You're not rushing down to the post." Jo's tone was more mild inquiry than outraged taxpayer so Liam didn't rise.

"I'm not officially on duty until next Monday."

"Are you going back out to take a look in that cave?"

"I thought I might." He waited.

"I think I'll follow you out there."

"I thought you might."

She flipped him off. Wy laughed.

"Jesus," Jo said, standing next to him at the top of the cliff.

"Yeah," Liam said, for once in complete agreement with her.

Her vehicle and Liam's truck were squeezed in next to Erik's old Ford. The sky was cloudy but at least it wasn't raining yet. He hesitated, and then shrugged. He turned sideways to the slope and began side-stepping down, digging the edges of his boots into the ground. Even then he slid almost halfway there, but at least it was a more controlled slide than Monday's. Above him, Jo inched her way, sometimes by the seat of her pants, sometimes voluntarily.

He was dusting himself off when a bird called and he looked up to see a seagull cruising by, followed a second later by two more. No ravens, though.

The tent looked the same. The tables stood on either side

of the tent, the coffee table in one corner, the fold-up Styrofoam bed in another, the aged Blazo boxes converted to shelves containing the cleaned, neatly laid out tools of Erik's profession and the carefully labeled artifacts. The *Shawshank* rock hammer was still there.

"Erik?" Liam said. No answer. He raised his voice. "Erik?"

Behind him he heard a scatter of sand and rock. "It's easier going up than coming down," he said without turning.

"Good to know," Jo said breathlessly. "Berglund still not around?"

"Doesn't appear so."

"Have you checked the cave?"

"I was just about to." He pulled the tactical flashlight from the holster on his belt and led the way through the tent into the mouth of the cave.

The darkness of the cave gulped down the light of the flash and if possible made the interior look even darker and somehow larger than he had noticed on Monday. It was colder than he remembered, he thought fifty degrees at most. It smelled off, too, more than just of decaying seaweed. A chill ran down his spine and his heart sank.

He took a step forward toward what he guessed what the back of the cave and immediately tripped over something and fell to his knees. He dropped the flash and it went out. "Damn it." He groped for the flash, hoping it hadn't broken against the rock, hampered by being totally disoriented, only dimly aware of Jo's figure outlined against the light of the cave entrance. The dimensions of the cave seemed to expand exponentially in the dark.

"Liam?"

"Don't come in. The floor is a bunch of rock." He understood now why Erik hadn't walked him inside it during his visit. "Just stay there until I find the flashlight." His hand closed over it finally. He felt for the switch and pushed it.

It lit immediately, illuminating the face of Erik Berglund peering out from behind an outcropping of rock separated from the wall of the cave.

"Erik?"

But Erik's eyes were wide and staring. His blond hair was matted with what could only be dried blood.

Behind him Liam heard Jo take a sharp, inward breath.

"Stay there, Jo." He got to his feet and picked his way carefully to the little rock wall Erik's body had fallen—or been placed—behind.

He put out a hand. Erik's skin was cold and clammy to the touch.

Erik's right arm was outstretched over his shoulder. Liam traced it with the beam of the flash and saw a phone under his lifeless hand.

He bent to pull it free and straightened to thumb it on.

It was dead.

Like Erik.

Twelve

Wednesday, September 4

"RIGOR IS STARTING TO PASS OFF," LIAM said, "but the cave where the body was is pretty cool and I'd guess colder at night."

Brillo grunted. "Anybody around who can take a read?"

"No."

"You sure it wasn't an accident?"

"I can't tell, Brillo. I can say that his skull shifts when you touch it."

"He couldn't have fallen?"

"Not where the body is. I mean, yes, he could have tripped and fallen, there is plenty to fall over in the cave, but at least at first glance he looks like he's taken a lot of damage, more than could be reasonably expected from a trip-and-fall. His clothes, too."

"Well, shit." An aggravated sigh. "Put him on a plane."

"Don't hang up, Brillo, there's something else."

"Color me surprised." Dr. Hans Brilleaux, the state medical inspector, went heavy on the sarcasm.

"There is another body in the cave, a skeleton. Been there a while, just the bones. I can see it but I can't get at it yet. I do have one of the hands."

A huff of exasperation. "Send it up with the body."

"I want to know if it's human and how long it's been there, Brillo."

"Miracle workers R us." Click.

Liam lowered his phone.

"It takes thirty-six hours for rigor to go off," Jo said.

"This is now a crime scene, Jo. I need to ask you to leave."

"If he's been lying there for thirty-six hours, how did the boys miss him?"

"Jo."

"You and what army?" she said impatiently. "How are you going to get the body up that trail?"

He called the post. Ms. Petroff answered. He explained the situation. "I will notify the Blewestown volunteer fire department, sir."

"We're sure they will respond all the way out here?"

"The fire department always responds everywhere, sir," she said, the reproof clear in her tone.

"Thank you, Ms. Petroff."

Instead of hanging up in her usual efficient fashion, she said hesitantly, "Did I understand you to say that you were at the archeological dig up East Bay Road, sir?"

"You did."

"And the deceased?"

"We don't comment on ongoing investigations, Ms. Petroff."

A brief silence. "I see. Thank you, sir. I will so inform the fire department." Click.

He stared at his phone. In the entirety of his acquaintance with Ms. Petroff, all one and a half days of it, that was the first time she had requested clarification on any point at issue. Don't go soft on me now, Ms. Petroff, he thought, and called Wy. "Got a job for you, not a fun one."

"Do tell."

He was momentarily distracted by the husky quality of her voice but called himself sternly to order and to duty. "I've got a body that needs transporting to Anchorage. The ME's office will meet you at Merrill to take it off your hands."

"Height and weight?"

He had never loved her more. "Six foot plus, a hundred and sixty pounds or thereabouts. Maybe less, skinny guy."

"I'll head for the airport and start prepping the Cessna."

"Need a favor."

"Name it."

"Those hand bones from yesterday night. I want you to take those to Brillo, too."

"Sure. Where are they?"

"In my truck." He looked at Jo, who wasn't even pretending not to listen. "Jo will bring them to you."

"Now just a damn minute—"

"Of course," Wy said.

"Thanks, babe. Usual rates. I'll clear it through the office."

"Always a pleasure doing business with the state, Sergeant Campbell." She paused, and then said delicately, "Someone you know?"

"Unfortunately. One of two possible friends I've met since I got here. The archeologist."

"Oh." A sigh. "He sounded like a good guy. I'm sorry."

"Yeah. Later, babe."

"Tell Jo I'll meet her at the airport, and give her the gate code."

"Wilco." He clicked off and looked up to see Jo giving him a baleful stare. "You're all I've got, Jo. Please."

"And it gets me out of your crime scene."

He didn't deny it. "There is that."

She grumbled but she went. He spent the next twenty minutes photographing, measuring, and making notes of the scene with apps on his phone, hoping that Steve Jobs wasn't going to let him down. When the Blewestown volunteer fire department showed up they galloped down the trail like sherpas. It looked like the entire department had responded, a cross section of locals ranging in age from twenty to sixty, including a muscular, no-nonsense woman who introduced herself as Fire Chief Fiona Rafferty. "Campbell," she said. "Liam Campbell?"

"Yes."

"The shootout in the Newenham airport."

He repressed a sigh. "Yes."

"Not anyone's finest hour."

"No."

"But not your fault, either."

He almost smiled. "Thanks."

Rafferty and her men went to work. They knew what they were doing and had Berglund's body on a stretcher up the hill very nearly at double time. "Mountain goat DNA" was evidently one of the job requirements.

Liam pulled the chief to one side. "I need some help, Chief."

"Name it, Sergeant."

A refreshing relief from Chief Armstrong's determined indifference, and Liam was relieved. "A couple of kids were in this cave yesterday."

"They found the body?"

"No. Well, not this one."

Chief Rafferty had thick, expressive eyebrows and at this point they raised the brim of her ball cap by a quarter of an inch. "'This one?'"

"They were exploring and they found what they said was a crack that led to a cave behind this one. Evidently it is wide enough for one of them to get stuck in it and while he was stuck he found a skeleton. When they unstuck him he managed to grab the bones of one of the skeleton's hands."

Her eyebrows lowered to a level denoting extreme skepticism. "Sergeant Campbell—"

"I know, Chief. I've got the bones he recovered on the way to Anchorage to see if they are actually human bones.

But could you take a look at the crack and see if there is some way to reach the rest of the skeleton?"

"If it's that narrow how the hell would anyone get through it to die on the other side in the first place?" But she followed him, grumbling, and then retreated immediately to radio up the hill for one of her remaining cohort to bring down a couple of battery-powered standing lamps. "Need 'em for night fights sometimes," she said at his glance.

His phone dinged and he pulled it out to see that Wy had texted him.

> Taking off. Jo's coming with. Penis Extender parked
> at the tie-down, keys behind the visor.

He replied with a heart emoji and didn't care who saw it.

The lamps improved the view immeasurably, and for the first time Liam realized how big the cave was, the stygian darkness having swallowed so much of it before. Interested in spite of herself, Chief Rafferty joined him in his search, and even then the two of them working together, scrutinizing the rock surface with minute attention, almost missed it. It wasn't really a crack so much as a vertical separation of the cave's surface, one piece on top of another with a very narrow space between. "Kind of like a slip fault," Chief Rafferty said.

Liam didn't speak geology and was willing to take her word for it. He could well believe that Erik had never found the crack in spite of the time he'd spent on the dig and was even more astonished that Kevin and Logan had. Never underestimate the curiosity and determination of a ten-year-old kid. He could understand why they hadn't noticed Erik's body, too. They'd stumbled through the cave and fetched up against the back wall.

He hoped with all his heart that Brillo would find that Erik had died before they entered the cave.

They wrangled one of the lights over to the crack and leaned it against the rock wall, angling it as best they could to shine in between the two layers of rock. The separation wasn't even four inches in places, and try as he might he couldn't press his face flat enough against the rock to see to the other side. He stepped back, frustrated. "How did that kid get his head in that crack?"

"Wait," Rafferty said, and pulled out what looked like a dental mirror on a telescoping rod. She saw his look and shrugged and assumed a very bad British accent. "Rafferty. Jane Rafferty."

He laughed. He liked Chief Rafferty.

"Bought it off my dental hygienist. Useful for checking tight spaces." She got down on her knees and pressed her bulk up against the rock wall. She extended the mirror's handle out to its full length and poked it very slowly and very carefully through the crack. "Don't want to break it off."

"Don't want it to get stuck, either." Or her, he thought.

The cave seemed to be getting colder and the passing seconds stretched into minutes and maybe hours as Rafferty poked around with the mirror, working it like a surgeon doing a sextuple bypass, giving up only the occasional grunt.

Finally she sat back on her heels, collapsing the mirror. She stared at the crack, although without her hand actually inside it it faded again almost into invisibility. "Huh."

"Is there a skeleton?" Liam said. His toes were numb.

"Yes." She got to her feet.

"Could you tell if it was human or animal?"

"Oh, I think human. Let's go outside where it's warmer."

Even with a cloudy sky it felt infinitely warmer outside the cave. "Why human?"

"It's a human skull, Sergeant. I used to work arson investigation and I've seen a few. It's human, all right."

Liam drew in a breath and let it out on a long, expressive exhale. "Well, shit."

"Yeah."

"We have to get it out of there."

To her credit and his everlasting gratitude she didn't say, "What do you mean, 'we'?"

༷

The chief checked in with her people and they were to a man willing to play, probably because it meant that much more time away from their day jobs.

From a frankly unbelievable selection of tools, in the end they defaulted to a crowbar, a sledgehammer, and brute force. It didn't take as long as he expected before he was peering into a roughly round hole sharply edged with jagged rock. Rafferty moved the lamps so the light fell full onto the scene within.

"Fuck," one of the men said. "He's, like, totally mashed."

"Pulverized," another said.

"Pulped," said a third.

Not quite any of those things but not far off, Liam thought. With an inner sigh he got out his phone and opened the camera app to take more photos.

"Something's been chewing on him."

"What could get in there?"

"I don't know. Rats, I guess?"

"Do we even have rats in Baytown?"

"Maybe Rodents of Unusual Size?"

"Gary!"

"Jesus, dude, put a lid on it."

"Ever the class act, Feldman."

A brief silence, while everyone looked everywhere but at Liam and the chief.

"Cockroaches then," a subdued voice said. "Or bats, maybe?"

Everyone involuntarily looked up at the cave's ceiling.

"I've seen year-old bear kill with less damage."

"Chief, could I trouble you for another body bag?"

"Certainly, Sergeant. Garvey, would you do the honors?"

"Sure, Chief."

Liam stepped carefully through the hole, and wasted only a few blasphemous moments freeing a shoelace from a snag.

"Ought to get you some boots with Velcro fastenings, Sergeant. Easy on, easy off, and they don't catch on anything."

Liam crouched over the skeleton, taking more photos from every angle. He had a one-yard tape measure attached to his key chain. He ran it out next to the skeleton and took more photos. If this was a crime scene, the photos were the only crime scene evidence he would have.

Other than the skeleton itself. It was, as the firefighters had said, in ruins, all of the bones broken more than once and the skull broken in on both sides. Had the body been dismembered? He crouched down for a closer look. The hip, knee and elbow joints looked as if they might still have been intact when they were—What? Fell? Placed?—in the cave. They still fit together, or they would until he tried to pick them up.

He looked up, ignoring the faces peering in at him. The bones were just this side of the common wall between the two caves. He got down on one knee and took more photos.

He got to his feet again. The skeleton was pitiably small, about the size of the two boys who had discovered it. He didn't know how long these bones had been here but it was a given that someone had missed the person it had been, and it would be his job to find that someone or their relatives. If this proved to be a child, he might be dealing with parents, and certainly siblings. There was nothing worse in law enforcement life.

"Here's the bag, Sergeant."

"Thanks, Chief."

They watched in silence as he collected the bones and placed them in the bag and zipped it up. He cradled it in his arms and stood up. The bag weighed next to nothing. Chief Rafferty and her crew fell back as he stepped through the hole and formed a sort of guard of honor behind him as he toiled up the trail. At the top he laid the bag down gently in the backseat of one of their vehicles, and they drove in solemn procession back into town. Rafferty gave him a ride out to the airport to pick up his truck and he transferred the remains into the bed.

"Chief?"

"Sergeant?"

"Could you ask your people to keep this on the down low?"

She looked at him. "Those bones have been there a long time, Sergeant."

"Still."

She sighed and nodded. "I'll try."

"Thanks. By any chance, do you know where Erik Berglund lived?"

"Not a clue," she said.

They exchanged somber nods and she left him standing there, staring at the bag. It looked almost empty.

His phone dinged.

Delivery complete. Departing in five.

He looked from the screen back to the body bag.

Can you do a quick turnaround?

A beat.

You have another body you need transporting?

Well, she'd always been pretty quick.

The rest of the skeleton. The local fire chief and her
crew helped me get it out.

You're sure it's human then.

Unfortunately. I think it's a kid.

Be there in an hour, home again before dinnertime.

This time he responded with a gif that had Jim Carrey as
The Mask with his heart beating up out of his chest—he'd
been saving it up—and she returned a winky face with a
kiss.

He found a food cart out on the Spit with excellent fish
tacos, although a handmade sign warned him they were
closing as soon as they'd emptied out the freezer. "We don't
serve freezer-burnt fish," the proprietor informed him, "so
we don't close until everything we bought this year is sold."

In that case he went back for seconds. Satisfied in both
body and spirit he pulled through the gate at the airport at

the exact moment Wy landed. She taxied to the tie-down, killed the engine, and stepped down from the cabin and into his arms. She felt good there. She felt necessary.

"It'll be okay, Liam," she said, snuggling into his chest. "You'll find out who they were and restore them to their family. There can't be anything worse than losing a kid." She went still. "I'm sorry, I—"

"Stop it. I knew what you meant and you couldn't be more right anyway." He put a hand beneath her chin to raise up her face and kissed her. After a moment she relaxed into it, and as always that longing that was never very far off simmer anyway came to its usual instantaneous boil.

She smiled against his mouth. "Hold that thought, Campbell."

"Text me when you're fifteen minutes out."

She saluted and did a quick walk-around to make sure nothing had fallen off the plane in between the time she took off from Anchorage and landed in Blewestown while he loaded the body bag into the plane. She climbed back in the Cessna and he closed the door behind her, watching through the window as she donned the headset and picked up the checklist. He stepped back and after a few moments the engine fired and the prop began to turn. She smiled at him and he stood there watching until she had lifted off again into the sky, as always making it look graceful and effortless.

Flying always looked so much better from the ground.

He got in his truck and drove back into town. When he turned onto Alder the first thing he saw was Sybilla Karlsen, making her way down the hill. At least this time she had her clothes on. He sighed, put the truck into park, and got out. "Hello again, Mrs. Karlsen." He doffed his cap.

With the erratic memory of someone who has lived a very long time, she knew him at once. "Sergeant Campbell." She patted her hair. "How nice to see you again. What brings you out on this beautiful day?"

He refrained from pointing to either the post half a block up the hill from where they were standing or the cloudy sky overhead, and said, "Just taking in the sights, ma'am. Yourself?"

For the first time she looked a little uncertain. "I was on my way home."

He indicated his truck with a sweep of his hand. "May I offer you a lift?"

She fluttered a little as her cheeks went pink. "Why, how kind, Sergeant. It's just up the hill from here."

"I remember, ma'am." He gave her a discreet boost into the passenger seat, whereupon she fluttered some more, and got back into the pickup and put it in gear. When they passed the post she said, "Oh yes, you have that nice young Sally Petroff working for you, don't you? Such a sweet girl. Pity about the tragedy. I always felt so sorry for Kimberley."

Liam stopped at the stop sign at Sourdough, waited for traffic, and proceeded across the intersection. "Tragedy, ma'am?"

"Young men can be so thoughtless, don't you agree?"

"I do," Liam said. They drew up in front of Sunset Heights,

to meet an attendant coming out of the door who looked relieved when she saw Sybilla. "Sybilla, you had us worried." She smiled at Liam over Sybilla's head. "Thank you..."

"Sergeant Liam Campbell, Alaska State Troopers. I met Mrs. Karlsen on the road and offered her a ride."

Sybilla fluttered her eyelashes and deepened her dimples. "Indeed, young man, you can give me a ride anytime."

The attendant and Liam grinned at each other over her head, and Liam drove back down to the post. Ms. Petroff was at her station, because of course she was. "Good morning, Ms. Petroff."

"You gave me to understand that you wouldn't be into the office again until Monday, sir."

It felt like a reprimand. Manfully, Liam shrugged it off. "What do you know of Erik Berglund, Ms. Petroff?"

There was an almost infinitesimal pause. "The archeologist, sir?"

He had the baseless feeling that she was buying time. He couldn't imagine why and dismissed the suspicion. "Yes."

She folded her hands on the desk, and then refolded them. "He was born in Kapilat. He lost both his parents when their crabber went down in the Bering. I believe he was eighteen at the time. He went Outside to school, after which he worked overseas for UNESCO at various archeological sites. This year he left UNESCO and returned home to the Bay, where he works at an archeological site he discovered."

"You can make a living at that?"

"It is my understanding that archeologists and their

projects subsist mainly on grants. It is why most of them have day jobs as teachers."

"Did Berglund?"

She shook her head. "Not here in Blewestown, although there was talk that he had been offered a position on the Chungasqak Bay Campus."

Liam rifled through the mental card index labeled "Blewestown" and came up empty. "Which is..."

"The local affiliate of the University of Alaska. About five hundred students, including distance students from across the Bay."

He spared yet another moment to marvel at the comprehensiveness of Ms. Petroff's knowledge of her community. Well, theirs, now. "Was Berglund married?"

A shadow passed so fleetingly across her face that he could not identify the emotion behind it. "Not to my knowledge."

"A steady girlfriend?"

A ghost of a smile. "If the rumors are true, he did not lack for female companionship."

"Terrific," Liam said beneath his breath. He foresaw a lot of interviews with ex-girlfriends and those never went well and were almost invariably unproductive.

"Sir?"

"Yes, Ms. Petroff?"

"You are referring to Mr. Berglund in the past tense."

He looked up to find her watching him, her face blank of any expression, even curiosity. "Do you know where he lived, Ms. Petroff?"

Another almost imperceptible pause. "I believe he rented a dry cabin somewhere out East Bay Road."

"No address?"

She shook her head. "Dry cabins seldom have their own street addresses. People out that way throw up a lot of cabins for short-term rental purposes. They would rather not attract the attention of the borough tax assessor."

"What is a dry cabin, exactly?"

"No water. He had to haul it in."

"Ugh."

"It's not uncommon in Blewestown, sir, given the lack of housing. Many rental property owners rent out by way of Airbnb during the summer. Short-term vacation rentals are much more remunerative—" he could only admire how she didn't stumble over the word "—than long-term rentals."

Newenham had been the same, except replace tourists with the fishermen and the processing plant workers who flooded in from Outside every summer.

He thought it over. His first stop should have been Erik's office, but he hadn't had one. His second stop would have been Erik's home, but he didn't want to waste his entire day stumbling around the back of beyond trying to find it. "Do you by any chance have Gabe McGuire's phone number?"

"Of course, sir." A brief clack of keys and she read it off to him.

To his surprise, McGuire answered his own phone. "Mr. McGuire, this is Sergeant Campbell."

"Hey, Liam," McGuire said. He didn't sound happy. "I suppose this is about Erik."

"You've heard?"

A snort. "You're not from around here, are you?"

Neither are you, Liam thought. "I need to talk to you about your party on Monday. In particular it would be helpful if you could prepare a list of everyone who was invited, who was there, and who didn't show."

"I suppose this is official?"

"Yes."

A heavy sigh. "I'm not a law enforcement officer but I've played one in the movies. Come on out."

"Thanks. Be there in twenty." Liam clicked off. "Thank you, Ms. Petroff. Excellent staff work."

She inclined her head and said gravely, "Thank you, Sergeant Campbell."

He paused at the door to look back at her. She was still looking at him with that preternaturally blank expression. He couldn't tell what she was thinking. He wasn't sure she actually saw him.

Thirteen

Wednesday, September 4

BY THIS TIME HIS TRUCK COULD HAVE driven itself to its destination, but for the black bear and three cubs who charged out in front of it with suicidal intent. He slammed on the brakes and got honked at by the pickup in back of him for his pains. The bears, unconcerned, disappeared into the brush. They were as adept at the vanishing act as the moose.

The gate had been left open. He parked and knocked at the door. McGuire opened it almost immediately. "Coffee?"

"Sure."

McGuire pointed at the kitchen and Liam helped himself. They sat down on opposite couches in the living room, McGuire facing the view as was only due the homeowner.

"Do you live here alone?"

McGuire looked around. "What, too much room for one guy?" He sounded defensive.

Liam shook his head. "You're an actor. And you're a box office star. Where's the entourage?"

McGuire grimaced, and Liam admitted that it was very odd indeed to watch a face he'd seen often on his own television screen make human expressions sitting right across from him. Liam was generally good at spotting liars and their tells but this guy was a professional actor, the first and only of Liam's acquaintance. How to know what was real?

McGuire looked back at Liam, and something of his thoughts must have shown because—was it an expression of disgust—flashed across his face. He hooked a thumb over his shoulder. "There's a cabin out back. Len lives there. A housekeeper comes once a week. The rest of the time it's just me."

"Was Len at the party?" A nod. "I'd like to talk to him, too."

"Want me to call him over?"

"No, I'll pay a visit afterward." He wanted to talk to the witnesses individually if at all possible.

"Right," McGuire said. He picked up a sheet of paper from the coffee table. "I printed it out. Easier to read than my handwriting." He fidgeted with it. "I don't mean to intrude on your investigation but these people were my guests, in my home by my invitation. I don't want to hang them out to dry." He looked up to meet Liam's eyes.

"I appreciate your feelings," Liam said. "My on-the-scene estimate indicates that Erik Berglund was killed late Monday or early Tuesday morning. That estimate is not official and may be contradicted by the findings of the medical examiner, but if it's close then you and your party guests will have been the last to see him alive."

"Other than the murderer," McGuire said. "Who wasn't necessarily here."

Liam nodded his totally deniable agreement. You never got the best out of a witness by antagonizing them right out of the chute. "Did everyone you invited come?"

"Yes." McGuire handed over the sheet of paper. Erik Berglund's name was at the top of the list. Next were Allan and Cynthia Reese and Grace and Greg Kinnison. "Kyle and Logan's parents?"

McGuire nodded.

Aiden and Shirley Donohoe. Domenica Garland. Hilary Houten. Blue Jay Jefferson. Jeff and Marcy Ninkasi. Allison Levy. Jake and Lily Hansen. Paula Pederson. Alexei and Kimberley Petroff.

"Do Alexei and Kimberley Petroff have a daughter named Sally?"

"I don't know."

"Was your friend Len present?"

McGuire nodded.

"What's his full name?"

"Leonard Needham."

Liam counted the names. "And you makes twenty. Just a holiday get-together? Any excuse to barbecue?"

McGuire looked uncomfortable, but Liam couldn't tell if he actually felt that way or just wanted Liam to think he felt that way. "Some of them are neighbors. Jeff and Erik are friends. The rest are local people. I invited them over for a kind of home premiere of *Last Flight Out*." If Liam couldn't read his expression he could read Liam's, and he added, "The producer sent me an answer print."

He might as well have been speaking in tongues but Liam did manage to gather that McGuire had invited everyone over to watch his next film.

A reluctant smile spread across McGuire's face. "Not a fan?"

"More of a reader."

A rough laugh made both of them look at the kitchen where a man was filling a mug with coffee. He brought it to the living room and sat down next to McGuire. "Leonard Needham. You'd be the trooper." Liam nodded, and the man jerked his head at McGuire. "Kid told me you'd be coming. Thought I should come on over to make sure you don't get out the rubber hose." He waggled his considerable eyebrows and his cheeks creased in a close-mouthed smile. White, five seven-eight with a kind of muscular thinness that defied an estimate of weight. His eyes were brown with startlingly long lashes and his hair was a wiry gray cut to a drill instructor's specifications. His hands were enormous and large-knuckled, dwarfing the mug he held. He was dressed like McGuire, in a worn white T-shirt advertising nothing and jeans faded at the knees and seams. He was also twice McGuire's age, and although the two men looked nothing alike there was a certain similarity in the way they held themselves, a quality of awareness, Liam thought. Perhaps the consciousness that there was always someone watching, which would be endemic in people employed in the on-camera end of filmmaking. He recognized it because nowadays if you were in law enforcement you were always aware that someone was watching, usually with their camera phone up and running.

"Generally speaking, we don't break out the rubber hose until the second interview," he said. Needham bent his head, acknowledging the unspoken reproof. Both men wore almost identically bland expressions and Liam said, "Are you an actor like Mr. McGuire, Mr. Needham?"

"It's Len, and call him Gabe," Needham said. "And no, I'm not an actor, I work for a living."

McGuire might have rolled his eyes a little.

Liam reminded himself that this was an official interview regarding a murder committed very likely not a thousand feet from where he sat and managed not to smile. "What do you do, Len?"

"I'm a stunt man. Or I was."

"Nowadays he's my pilot," McGuire said.

"And this punk's uncle, for my sins."

Liam gave up and let himself be distracted. "How did you get into that?"

Len correctly identified which part of his life Liam was asking about and said, "I'm a pilot. I was two tours in the Air Force, did time in the Sandbox, got out when the hypocrisy got to be a little too much. A friend already in the business was working on a film that needed a stunt pilot right now and the money was good." He shrugged.

"Ten years later he owned his own company, and then he recruited me out of high school."

"Kid played every sport. Coulda gone pro."

"Boring," McGuire said.

"And then…"

McGuire gave a shrug identical to the one Needham had just given and the similarity between the two shifted into a sudden focus that was so startling that Liam was amazed he hadn't seen it before. "A director gave me a line, and in his next film a couple more, and then a supporting role in a film that got some traction at Sundance, and then, and then." He drank coffee. "It's all luck, really. Plenty of actors better than me didn't get the breaks." He looked at his uncle. "Didn't have Len."

"Stop it, kid, you're making me blush." He pointed at Liam with his mug. "And it's not what you came here to talk to us about."

"Erik." Gabe sat back with a sigh. "Damn it."

"Why damn it?" Liam said.

Gabe met Liam's eyes squarely. "He was a friend."

Len snorted again. "He wasn't always." When Gabe glared at him Len glared right back. "Tell him. Tell him right now, tell him all of it. Otherwise he'll find out from someone else and he'll be back here all pissed off and suspicious because you didn't. It's not like you haven't made that picture, kid."

Gabe dropped his head. "Fuck." He looked up at Liam.

"Fine. This house is in a subdivision called Bay View. Yeah, I know, original as hell. The trail to Erik's dig has been public for a long time, people driving down to park at the roundabout and rappel down to walk on the beach. It isn't officially a public right of way but it's been used as one. The neighbors tell me it's an historic make-out spot for the local teens and lately it's been a problem area for raves."

"Define 'problem.'"

"Drug deals. Underage drinking. Accidents originating therefrom—you've experienced the grade. Imagine you're a dumb kid and high or drunk besides. ODs and even a few deaths back in the day." Gabe rubbed the heels of his hands against his eyes. "And then along comes Gabe McGuire, the rich and famous Outsider, who buys the house right next door and, worse, moves in. Word gets around, rubbernecker traffic increases, the neighbors are unhappy."

"Made even more so when Erik Berglund sets up an archeological dig at the foot of the trail," Len said, with a glance at Gabe. "Because Erik is bent on establishing a traditional Alaska Native trail leading from the beach up the hill and all the way over the bluff, that he is going to prove has been used ever since there have been Alaska Natives living in the Bay. Which would be, give or take, ten thousand years. You'll have noticed the rocky spur that runs out of the cliff and down the beach. Makes kind of a natural harbor."

"He gave me the tour," Liam said.

"In the meantime," Gabe said, looking a little clenched around the jaw, "the rich and famous Outsider has approached the Borough to vacate the trail right of way in exchange for putting in another, more accessible trail, at his own expense, on the right of way between this subdivision and the next one south of here, Mountain View. Another exemplar of originality in binomial nomenclature."

This time Len rolled his eyes. "Forgive the kid. Every now and then he reads a book and wants to make sure everybody knows it."

Liam's eyes raised involuntarily to the bookshelf that covered the entirety of one wall, floor to ceiling. There were no empty spaces, and all the covers were worn. "So you were trying to vacate the right of way to the beach."

"This one, yeah." Gabe shifted uncomfortably. "There have been some incidents."

"What the kid means and is too embarrassed to say is that fans today have no boundaries, women fans in particular."

"What about the gate? Don't you close it?"

"They climb over it. One of them took the trail down to the beach, walked down it a ways, climbed back up to the edge of the cliff—" Len nodded at the yard which ended at the cliff's edge "—and came over the top, herself in the altogether. If she'd managed to pack a platter with her I reckon she would have served herself up on it."

"You mean she was naked?"

"Yep. I'll never understand why she didn't leave her clothes on for the climb and just strip after she got to the top. She sure was scratched up in some interesting places. I have no objection to naked women, mind you, but that was not a sight you want to see over your first cup of coffee in the morning."

"Jesus."

"Yeah."

Liam digested this in silence for a moment. "So your plan was to vacate the right of way—"

"There is no right of way, not officially."

"Hard to make that stick with umpteen generations of people who have been using it for whatever," Len said.

"And then," Liam said slowly, "along comes Erik Berglund, who says the trail might go back millennia for the Sugpiaq."

Gabe nodded glumly. "And if he's right, there will be zero chance of me gaining title to that trail."

"And now he's dead."

It was his turn to be glared at. "I can always buy another house."

"Yeah, but you like this one," Len said.

Gabe transferred his glare. "Whose side are you on anyway?"

Len patted the air. "Relax, kid. Better the trooper knows it all upfront."

Gabe crossed his arms and glared out the window instead. "I liked Erik, right of way or no right of goddamn way. If he'd proved his point we could have come up with a workaround, and if not I would have learned to live with it. Maybe buy out the property on the other side of mine and put in access that way, and then close off the existing driveway altogether."

"Maybe build a moat while you were at it."

"Maybe," Gabe said with emphasis. He looked back at Liam. "I'm a full-time resident now, except when I'm off on a shoot. I'm here for the duration, registered to vote in Alaska and everything. No way I wanted to start out in the Bay with something like this." He sighed and let his arms fall. "Erik was a good person, and a scholar. I only knew him a couple of months but I think... I think we were on our way to being friends. I don't know that many people who don't give a shit who I am." He looked back at Liam. "And now we are all deprived of whatever future discoveries he might make, whatever they were and however they impacted me. Whoever killed him robbed us all. I hope you find him and throw him in prison for the rest of his life."

Liam looked down at the list. "When did the party start?"

"I told everyone six o'clock for food and drink. We ran the film at eight p.m. It ended at nine-thirty. There was dessert, more drinks, and everyone left between ten-thirty and eleven."

"No wait staff? No caterer?"

A shake of the head. "It was just beer and wine and burgers and dogs and ice cream."

"Who was the last to leave?"

"Erik," Gabe said glumly. "We had another beer and shot the breeze for another half an hour after everyone else left. You're right, Len and I are probably the last people to see him alive."

"After which," Len said, "the two of us cleaned up—"

He caught Liam's look and grinned. "Well, okay, we didn't actually clean up. We bagged the trash and stacked the dirty dishes. The housekeeper came the next morning and cleaned up."

"After that?"

"I went to bed."

"In your cabin?" Len nodded. Liam looked at Gabe. "And you?"

"I read for a while, then same."

"Do either of you know where Erik's cabin is?"

Both men shook their heads.

"I saw a fold-up bed in the tent. He spend the night there often?"

"I don't know about often. Sometimes he worked late."

Liam thought about taking that trail up in the dark and shuddered inwardly. "You think he slept there Monday night?"

Gabe's expression was bleak. "I don't know."

"You didn't see Erik's body in the cave when you went down to help Kyle?"

Gabe shook his head. "All I had was a flashlight and not a very big one. That cave is creepy enough during the day. I went straight in and straight out again."

"You didn't smell anything?"

Gabe's mouth tightened. "Place smelled like cave and I was focused on getting Kyle unstuck. If I'd noticed anything odd I would have said so, Sergeant." He emphasized the last word.

Liam thought about that for a minute. Between Kyle and Logan and Gabe, the cave had been like Grand Central Station that night. Still, as he now knew himself, it was a big space with a lot of obstruction to eyesight and foot traffic. He'd only found Erik Berglund's body because he'd tripped over the rocky surface. "I've already heard he pissed off a lot of people locally. Were any of them here that night?"

"The Reeses and the Kinnisons were pissed at him for gumming up the works with the right of way. He might have had a thing with Domenica Garland, who is also a neighbor, a couple doors up."

Len snorted. When Liam looked at him he said, "Ain't no male in the room that night Domenica Garland hasn't had a thing with. She is busy, that girl."

"Including the two of you?"

Len laughed. "I don't have anything she wanted."

"Bullshit," Gabe said, "you just run faster than the average man."

"And you, Gabe?"

"I have a pretty good turn of speed myself," Gabe said.

In spite of himself Liam grinned. "I've met the lady. I can relate." He looked back at the list. "What about the rest of your guests?"

"Some I've met and liked. Some I met and wanted to get to know better for other reasons."

"Alexei and Kimberley Petroff?"

"He's the chief of the local tribe. I met him when I took

the boat over to Kapilat on Memorial Day, and he was on this side for the Labor Day weekend, so..." He shrugged.

A friendly acquaintance with the chief of the most powerful local tribe would not be a bad thing for any bigwig who moved into the area. Liam mentally commended the actor on his diplomatic instincts.

"Did any of them get in an argument with Erik that evening?"

McGuire and Needham exchanged glances. Needham said, "Erik and Hilary Houten were arguing, but they always are. Were."

"What about?"

"Houten telling Erik he was full of shit and that his theories were crap. He was serious about it, I think. Erik seemed mostly to be egging him on."

"Anyone else?"

"Jesus fuck, how I hate this," McGuire said, staring into his mug.

Len said, "Erik got into a conversation with Kimberley Petroff. It looked pretty intense."

"Did anyone else see?" Like her husband?

Len shook his head. "I don't think so. They were out in the yard there—" he nodded his head at the window "—and it was getting dark by then."

"Anyone else?"

"Blue Jay Jefferson, maybe? But then he's cranky with everyone. And he's the one who separated Houten and Erik."

"Did you hear any traffic on the road after everyone left?"

"No. There's a lot of insulation in the form of shrubbery between the house and the driveway."

Gabe shook his head.

"Could you do me a favor? Could the two of you take some time over this list and give me a sense of who left in what order? Erik left last, okay, but who left first? And how much time between departures?"

The two men looked at each other and shrugged. "Sure."

They put their heads together over the list. After a little argument, they handed it back with numbers in front of all the names.

Liam stood up. "Thanks for your time." He folded the piece of paper and tucked it away. "You'll be around for a while?"

"This you telling us not to leave town, lawman?" Len said, drawling out the words like he was an extra in a Randolph Scott movie.

"It kind of is," Liam said. He pulled on his cap and nodded. "Later, gentlemen."

Fourteen

Wednesday, September 4

LIAM SAT IN HIS PICKUP FOR FIFTEEN minutes, on the phone with Ms. Petroff. He read down the list for her and she gave him everyone's addresses and phone numbers. The Reeses and the Kinnisons were nearest but no one was home at either house. Probably everyone was at work and school. Liam left his card in the door jambs of both. He'd call them later.

After Kinnison and Reese was Domenica Garland, who lived in a Teutonically square house with one steep roof whose peak nearly achieved low earth orbit. It was shingled with large squares of dull black slate. At that angle if one of those suckers slid off it could decapitate Liam with one slice. The trees here all kept a safe distance as if they were thinking the same thing.

He got out of the truck and was startled by a flock of

barn swallows swooping back and forth through the air. It was September, not the height of mosquito season, and he wondered what they were eating.

He'd never given a damn about birds or bothered to learn their names and habits until a raven had started stalking him in Newenham. He needed to stop jumping every damn time something shook a tail feather at him.

He walked up a wide path made of more slices of slate, these a rusty gold in color. The slate continued up the broad low steps that led to an enormous wooden door that looked as if it had been looted from a Gothic cathedral. He pressed the ornate wrought iron doorbell, disappointed when he heard only one low, drawn-out "bonnngggg." By rights there should have been a rope with Quasimodo on the other end of it.

The door opened and, yes, it was the looker from the Backdraft parking lot. "Yes?" she said.

"Domenica Garland?"

"Yes. And you are?"

"I'm Sergeant Liam Campbell with the Alaska State Troopers, ma'am," he said, producing his badge, and smiling his very best smile. He was certain she would expect such a smile from every single man she met. "I wonder if you could spare me a few moments."

"What's this about?" she said, not budging.

"May I come in?" He took a step forward.

She fell back with a frown and even that looked good on her. He'd never seen hair and eyes that matched before, the black of ebony, of sunless space, of the slate on the roof. Of the inside of Erik's cave. She played it up, too; every article of clothing was black as well, button-down tucked into jeans, belt, shoes. As in the parking lot on Monday, everything fit her body so creaselessly that he could have speculated about her underwear. But he was better than that.

She probably wouldn't know it but the shoes were a dead giveaway that she wasn't from around here. All Alaskans kicked their shoes off at the door. Christmas at Grandma's house, the entryway looked like a shoe store.

The interior of this house looked the farthest thing from a shoe store, and the farthest thing from Grandma's house for that matter. The windows were floor-to-ceiling and wall-to-wall, and if there was a contest to who had more square feet of glass she would have beaten him and Wy and Gabe McGuire and Jeff's brewpub all together. The view was of course spectacular because it seemed every view in Blewestown was and because he had the feeling that this woman never settled for less than the best.

Next to the view, the rest of the house shouldn't have mattered but it was obvious that it did to the person who had built it. Most of it was covered in stone. There was a sort of navy blue slate on the floor, the countertops were brown speckled granite, the backsplash was white marble, and the fireplace surround was a broad strip of—amethyst? The hearth was a block of rose quartz, and the fireplace mantel and the windowsills were green jade.

It was Moria. It was the Hall of the Mountain Kings. It was the mine of the Seven Dwarves. "Dig, dig, dig, with a shovel and a pick," Liam said.

"I beg your pardon?"

"What a spectacular room," he said, smiling again as hard as he could.

Her eyes narrowed. "I know you, don't I?"

"Not formally, no. We, ah, passed in the parking lot of the brewpub on Monday."

"Oh. Ah. Yes. What's up, Sergeant? I don't begin every day with a visit from the troopers." She checked her phone. "I don't have long, I'm afraid. I have a meeting in town in half an hour."

She hadn't asked him to sit and he had a lively enough sense of self-preservation not to allow himself to get too comfortable in this house. "It's not good news, I'm afraid. Erik Berglund is dead."

She went very still for a moment. "But I just saw him Monday night."

"Yes, I know. It's why I'm here."

"But he's only forty years old."

"Yes. His death was not from natural causes."

Her eyes widened a fraction but otherwise she gave nothing away. "You mean someone killed him?"

"Yes."

Her disbelief was manifest. "Murder?"

"Unfortunately."

"Why would anyone bother?"

The invaluable Ms. Petroff had provided a thumbnail bio. Thirty-eight, unmarried, no children, graduated with a degree in civil engineering, had spent all her working life with RPetCo in Asia and South America, now head of operations in Alaska. Maybe she was just that cold. He made a pretense of consulting the notes app on his phone. "You were one of the guests at Gabe McGuire's party Monday evening."

"So was Erik."

"Yes, and preliminary evidence suggests that he died last Monday night or early Tuesday morning. Which makes the guests at the party the last people to see him alive."

"Other than the murderer."

"Other than the murderer," he said with a nod. "I understand that you had a personal relationship with Mr. Berglund."

"I did."

He waited. So did she. "Would you care to elaborate?"

"We were occasional bed partners," she said. "It was never more serious than that."

"How long did it last?"

"A month, perhaps."

"Was it over?"

She shrugged. "It is now. Obviously."

He was a little taken aback and tried not to show it. "Did you quarrel?"

Her smile was sharp and beautiful, although her dark eyes retained a perceptible wariness. "We had our differences."

"Because you're the head of RPetCo, and because RPetCo wants to drill for oil in Chungasqak Bay, and Erik might have thrown a stumbling block in your way?"

"Primarily. But Erik posed a very minor threat. The state of Alaska has always looked favorably on resource extraction."

Given the amount of money RPetCo donated in local elections, that was a given. "And your fields on the North Slope are drying up."

She nodded. "And, as you say, our fields on the North Slope are drying up."

"Did the two of you meet here? Or in town?"

She smirked. "Here. Obviously."

"Why obviously?"

"He was living in a dry cabin. I don't do dry cabins."

Liam glanced at the amethyst hearth. "Obviously." Her eyes narrowed. "Do you know where his cabin is?"

"No."

"When did you leave the party Monday night, Ms. Garland?"

"Domenica, please." She strolled forward, so far as he could tell solely so he could get a whiff of her perfume. "I arrived at six on the dot and left at ten-thirty, also on the dot. I was the first to leave."

"You're very exact."

"I'm a scheduler, Sergeant. I had to be home by eleven because I had a phone call scheduled with London then, which is eight a.m. their time." She held up her phone. "I keep everything on my calendar, should you require data to back up my word."

"I don't think that's necessary just yet." He tacked on the last two words just to see her reaction. There was none. A very cool customer, Domenica Garland. "I appreciate your time, Ms. Garland. I may need to get back to you with more questions as the case progresses. May I have your phone number?" He held up his phone in his left hand, making sure his wedding ring was clearly visible. It didn't even register on her peripheral vision.

"Of course." They exchanged numbers.

"Thank you. You'll be in state for the foreseeable future?"

She smiled but she didn't call him on it the way Len had. "I will." She waved a hand at the surrounding house. "This is my home, Sergeant. My permanent residence. I travel all over the state and Outside and overseas as well with my job, but I always come home again."

"Thank you," he said again, touching the brim of his cap. "I'll be in touch."

She smiled into his eyes. "I'm looking forward to it."

On the whole, he thought, as he turned the key in the ignition, he preferred flirting with Sybilla Karlsen.

His phone buzzed with incoming text.

Just turned the corner at Cook's Point. Ten minutes out.

It was after four and he felt he'd put in a hard day's work. He texted back a thumbs up and headed into town.

She had brought takeout from Moose's Tooth in Anchorage. As a bonus, she hadn't brought Jo back with her. "I think she means to hound Brillo about the autopsy."

Excellent news on many different fronts. Brillo was generally impervious to pressure but Jo was her own PSI of power tool. Liam might get results sooner than he'd hoped for. Plus, the best pizza in the world. Plus Wy.

But after dinner he felt a little restless, unable to concentrate on the book in progress, which was a shame because it was Simon Winchester's *Pacific* and like all Winchester's books informative and challenging and in some unspecifiable way he felt reading them made him a better law enforcement officer. Nevertheless, tonight he couldn't track. He closed it and said, "Want to go for a ride?"

Wy, who was reading what looked like a space opera on the other end of the couch, looked up and smiled. "Take a look around your new domain?"

"Not exactly."

They piled into his pickup and wandered around, first downtown, which existed largely between two parallel main streets, Sourdough and Cheechako, with others, all of them named for trees, intersecting them both perpendicularly. "Almost a perfect grid," Wy said.

The few restaurants still open were closed for the day, as were the coffee shops. Wy made sure to point out the bookstore, and they took note of the building supply store and the mini-mall that ran from a hardware store on one end to a quilt shop on the other. "We might never need to order anything by mail again," Wy said.

"Yeah." Liam headed back up Alder, crossed Sourdough, and continued up the face of the bluff, which remained paved all the way to the top, but with a steady increase in switchbacks that became more acute the higher they went. "I'm getting seasick," Wy said.

The road emerged at the edge of the bluff to intersect with another two-lane road that ran along the edge in either direction. The street sign said Heavenly View Drive, and it wasn't wrong, which they knew since they lived on it. "Right or left?" They had yet to explore beyond their new house in that direction.

"Left is home." Wy pointed up the Bay. "Right." That way she could admire the view, and he wouldn't have to endure the occasionally straight drop off the edge of the road. At least not until they drove back this way to get home.

The road had no shoulders but fortunately very little traffic. Driveways led to everything from log cabins covered in moss to McMansions that looked as if they'd been airlifted in from Orange County. He instructed Wy on the meaning of "dry cabin". She shuddered. "I lived my first year in Newenham with an outhouse. Don't ever want to do that again."

"Never had to, never want to. Ahah."

"Ahah what?"

He slowed, checked for traffic, and turned left on Baranov Avenue. "Ahah, this is the street Judge DeWinter lives on."

The surface was dirt and the sides were lined with an impenetrable hedge of alders that in places met overhead to form a tunnel. Roads with names like Shelikov and Rezanov appeared and disappeared along with the houses built on them. At one point the road went down one side of a steep if brief canyon, crossed a one-lane steel bridge with no railings over a dry creek bed, and climbed back up the other side. The landscape opened suddenly on what appeared to be a—yes, it was, a junk yard. There were dozens of cars, a black Ford F-150 with its cab smashed almost flat onto the seat, a gray Impreza with a crumpled hood and four flat tires, an old station wagon with wooden doors, and more of the same. The vehicles, if they could still be called that, were parked haphazardly on both sides of the road, leaving barely enough room for him to creep by. More had been dumped on the side of the road and left long enough to sprout fireweed through the broken windows.

"They better never have a fire at the end of this road," Wy said.

Liam thought of Chief Rafferty, and wondered if she'd ever been back here. Maybe she should pay it a visit. Maybe someone should tell her she should.

A two-story house with a flat roof and plywood siding stood adjacent to the junk yard. There was a soggy-looking couch next to a tire swing hanging from a deck that protruded from the second story, and an American flag over one window. On that deck stood a skinny guy in a MAGA cap taking a leak. He saw them and waved hello with his penis, creating a sparkly arc that showered the pit bull barking ferociously at them from the yard below.

"Ew," Wy said.

Liam slid past, just managing not to scrape the paint from the driver side of his pickup or to do a ditch dive off the other side of the road. The road began to incline and about ten yards down the alders closed in again. There were three more driveways off to either side and in half a mile the road ended at a two-story house with an attached garage and a view across Cook Inlet that included all the volcanoes from Douglas to Spurr.

"Spectacular," Wy said. "Is this the judge's house?"

"Yeah. Long commute."

"Worth it."

There was a turnout before the judge's driveway and Liam pulled around and headed back up the dirt road. The weenie wagger had disappeared, lucky for them.

"You can see why she's annoyed."

"I checked," Liam said. "There are no covenants in this subdivision. They can do what they want on their own property. The road, however, is maintained by the borough, and by ordinance they can't impede the right of way."

Wy chuckled. "I can hear you getting your ticket book out."

They pulled up at the stop sign. "Heavenly View Drive," Liam said.

"Trite but true," Wy said. "And we live right on it." She leaned over to kiss him. "This might just work out, Campbell."

He grinned all the way home.

Fifteen

Thursday, September 5

THE BLEWESTOWN CHAMBER OF COMMERCE opened at nine and Liam walked in the door at nine-oh-one and was still late to the party. Someone was giving a speech in front of a crowd of about fifty people. Liam remained beside the door to watch over everyone's heads. It was a large room with a desk in front of a door leading to offices in the back. The floor had a tiled representation of Chungasqak Bay on it with a Disney orca frolicking in the water. As appeared to be chronic with Blewestown construction, a wall of windows overlooked the Bay, with an adjacent wall covered in acrylic holders filled with brochures advertising halibut fishing, flightseeing, hotels and B&Bs, restaurants, art galleries and gift shops. Beneath it a newspaper dispenser made out of shellacked plywood held a stack of that year's *Visitor's Guide*.

The speaker was a man, early fifties, brown/brown, medium height, thickening around the middle. His scalp gleamed through a thin combover in the overhead lights. He wore a sports jacket that was one size too small over a button-down and jeans. Like at least half of the people in the room he wore Xtratufs. They appeared to be part of the civic uniform.

He was speaking with enthusiasm, so much so that an already high voice threatened to reach Mickey Mouse territory, but most of the time he managed to rein it in to a level audible to the human ear. "So, ladies and gentlemen, join me in thanking our very own Blue Jay Jefferson for making this incredible donation of $50,000 to the Blewestown Chamber of Commerce!"

There was a round of applause, although the man in front of Liam said to the woman standing next to him, "Blue Jay didn't even let Berglund get cold in his grave."

"He's going to piss off everyone on the south side of the Bay for sure."

"Been doing that for years."

"Why has he got such a hard-on for drilling in the Bay, anyway?"

"Who the hell knows? Maybe he owns stock in RPetCo."

Liam wondered why a big donation to the Blewestown Chamber of Commerce should piss off everyone on the Bay who didn't live in Blewestown.

An informal sort of receiving line formed as the applause died and as it did Liam could see the object of all the attention.

He recognized him immediately as the old fart with the walker he'd seen on the street on Monday, trying to kill the protesters with laser beams from his eyes. He'd also been at Backdraft. Liam watched as he shook everyone's hand and called them by their first names and asked after their children and grandchildren and brushed off any attempt to compliment him on his generosity. "Aw hell, come on now. It ain't much but it's what I can do."

The room began to empty out and Liam saw another man standing next to Jefferson, and he recognized him, too. It was the old man who had accompanied Domenica Garland to Jeff's pub. Hilary Houten, that was it. Houten looked a lot like Blue Jay Jefferson but that might have been because both men were in a similar state of decay. Old people always stood out in Alaska because there were so few of them. Alaskan winters weren't kind to old bones and retirement turned a lot of them into snowbirds. They'd come back just long enough to not lie on their Permanent Fund Dividend applications and head Outside again, for Oceanside or Sun City or Tampa, where it never snowed and sunrise and sunset stayed the same damn time year round, or near enough as not to keep you up all the damn night. Those who had managed not to blow everything they'd earned during the years of big oil spent their winters in Kona, which along about January seemed like a good idea to Liam, too.

All three men had been present at McGuire's party on Monday night.

The door closed behind the last person who wasn't Liam

and he walked forward. "I'm guessing you are Aiden Donohoe," he said. "Sergeant Liam Campbell, Alaska State Troopers. I'm in charge of the new post."

"Of course, of course," Donohoe said heartily, grabbing Liam's hand. His was damp and a little slippery and Liam was able to slide right out of it. He looked at the old man on Donohoe's left. "Mr. Jefferson."

"Sergeant. We howdied at Jeff's but we ain't shook. Call me Blue Jay. Everyone does." The bony hand was covered in papery skin and had a surprisingly strong grip, and his voice was surprisingly deep. "This here's a buddy of mine, Hilary Houten. He's got some fancy dan degree in old bones. For forty years I been telling him to get a real job but he's even better at ignoring me than he is looking at bones."

"Everybody's good at ignoring you, Blue Jay, and a good thing, too."

Hilary Houten's hand felt papery and fragile. Liam kept his grip gentle and released Houten's hand as soon as he could. "Nice to meet you again, gentlemen. I wonder if I might have a few moments of your time?"

"What can we do you for, Liam?" Donohoe said, but his eyes were wary.

He would rather have interviewed them separately, but the interaction between witnesses could also prove useful. "I'm guessing you've heard about Erik Berglund."

"Yes," Donohoe said. "Shame."

"Shame," Jefferson repeated, equally without conviction.

"Pudgy little fucker," Houten said, and thumped the end

of the diamond willow cane that was holding him up for emphasis. This close Liam could see that the handle had been inlaid with jade, and the striations of the bark were starkly dramatic. It really was a beautiful piece of work. If Liam ever needed a cane he wanted one exactly like that.

Then Houten's words caught up with him and he blinked, because Erik Berglund had been more lean and hungry than pudgy. "It appears that the last time Mr. Berglund was seen alive was at Gabe McGuire's party on Monday night. I understand that all three of you were in attendance."

Everyone waited for someone else to speak first. No one did. "Are any of you aware if Mr. Berglund had any enemies? Anyone he had annoyed at work, for instance?"

Donohoe rolled his eyes, Jefferson maintained his glare, and Houten snorted. "He said he'd quit his job to come home, but if you check I bet you'll find they fired his ignorant little ass." Houten's voice was high and indignant and wavery in a way that Jefferson's was not.

"There was almost no one in the Bay area that Erik hadn't made an enemy of," Donohoe said.

"Including yourself, Mr. Donohoe?"

"It's Aiden, Liam, and sure, I was pissed off at him. Have you seen RPetCo's rig parked up the Bay?"

"Yes."

"We've got a once-in-a-lifetime opportunity to build a resource extraction industry in the Bay that will provide hundreds of jobs, which is not a small deal for a community our size. And if they actually find oil that could be thousands of jobs, direct and support, for decades. And then along comes goddamn Erik Berglund, insisting with literally zero proof that the Bay should be declared off limits to resource extraction of any kind at least until he can prove his thesis. For what? An old trail that might or might not have existed that isn't even in use now?"

"I did see some of the artifacts he had discovered," Liam said.

With obvious patience Donohoe said, "We all saw them, Liam, including Hilary here, who has a lot more time on the job than Erik had, and Hilary says they don't date back more than a century."

"Mr. Houten?"

"Two at the most," Houten said in his high, quavering voice, "but that's pushing it beyond the bounds of scientific credibility. We argued about it. He laughed at me." It was clear that the memory stung.

Liam, whose experience with science was more along the lines of crime scene investigations, didn't know enough to argue with Houten. "The night of the party," he said, "did Erik have any arguments with any of the other guests? A quarrel loud enough to draw attention?"

"Come on, boy," Jefferson said. He looked older than Houten and sounded younger, his voice deeper and steadier. "There was almost no one at the party that didn't have a beef with Erik. Boy might not have known his bones but he did know how to make enemies. Including the host." His stare was challenging.

"You mean about vacating the right of way that led to the beach and Mr. Berglund's dig? Yes, Mr. McGuire told me about that."

"Hah! I'll just bet he did. Those Outside slickers got every base covered and all the money in the world to pay for 'em."

"You don't think I should believe him?"

"Don't put words in my mouth, boy. Where'd you say you were from, anyway?"

"I didn't, sir, but Newenham, most recently."

"Hah! You born in Alaska?"

It was a question an Alaskan old fart always asked, always at the beginning of any acquaintance. Alaska old farts could and would bury you with time served. Even if you had been born in Alaska, they could always trump you by having been born in the Territory, with chapter and verse on statehood and how they didn't vote for it, although let the record show that in 1958 Alaskans did vote for statehood six to one. "No, sir, I was born in Germany. We didn't move here until I was two years old."

"Army brat?"

"Air Force."

"Hah." It was beginning to sound more like a verbal tic than a judgment and Liam relaxed a little. "You never served?"

"No. Law enforcement was more my style."

"You one a them flying troopers?"

"No." God forbid. "But I can handle an ATV pretty well."

He was going for the joke but Jefferson didn't take it

that way. "How about a boat?"

"Never owned one."

"Hah."

Liam judged the job interview over, and said, "Gentlemen, as I said, I'm investigating the death of Erik Berglund. He was, in fact, murdered."

"How?"

"His body is with the medical examiner in Anchorage. It may be that the guests of Mr. McGuire's party were the last to see him alive. Did anything unusual happen that evening? Did he argue with anyone there? Did he leave with someone?"

"He was still there when I left," Donohoe said, and the two old men nodded agreement. "Look, Liam, here's the thing. Yes, he pissed off, well, pretty much everyone in the Bay, including a bunch of husbands, but murder?" He shook his head. "Besides, killing fights don't generally show up around here until February, along with cabin fever."

"And sure as hell nobody at that party would do something so goddamn foolish," Jefferson said. "All of 'em got way too much to lose."

Hilary Houten thumped his cane in agreement.

He asked them when they'd left the party and checked their departure times against Gabe and Len's recollections. He didn't find any glaring discrepancies. Donohoe said he and his wife had driven straight home, and their two teenagers were still up when they got there. Jefferson said he and Houten had spent the night on Jefferson's boat, docked in the harbor, and the next morning gone across to Jefferson's home in Jefferson Cove. Liam repressed a sigh. "One more thing. Do any of you know where Berglund lived?"

"Had a dry cabin out the road," Jefferson said. "Don't know where."

"Well, thanks, gentlemen, I appreciate the time. If I have any more questions I'll be in touch. None of you are traveling anywhere anytime soon?"

All three looked annoyed. All three shook their heads. Liam thanked them again and left.

In his truck he sat and thought for a moment. Fifty thousand dollars was a lot of money, no matter how much you had to start with. On the other hand, a lot of old, wealthy people wrote a lot of big checks because they weren't going to take it with them. He thought of the conversation he'd overheard while the presentation was taking place, and wondered.

Sixteen

Thursday, September 5

WY SPENT HER MORNING TEST-DRIVING her new car around Blewestown and environs. She went all the way out East Bay Road, which dead ended in Konstantinovka, a small village of Old Believers, Russian Orthodox who had split from the mother church over the way the sign of the cross was made (or so Wy had read and didn't quite believe). After the split they had migrated from Russia to, among other places, Alaska. Konstantinovka was a charming town, a village really, with white-painted clapboard houses surrounding a beautiful Russian Ortho-dox church. The church had a blue and white dome with a gilt cross on top, and the double doors of the entrance were surrounded by painted mosaics of people with gilt halos. If the inside was as beautiful as the outside a congregant might be able to endure standing for the entirety of the three-hour ceremonies.

She turned without stopping and drove back to town, taking her time. It had been dark when she and Liam and Jo drove the road on Wednesday night. Today she could see that it ran halfway between the beach and the bluff. Homes were built on the shoulder of the road and at the foot of the bluff, with some perched on the very edge of the small bluff that sat at the water's edge. There were more than a few farms and she saw one with rolled bales of hay scattered around a newly shorn field. A nursery advertised a three-for-one sale on their remaining trees. A tank farm backed up a fuel oil business, there were half a dozen storage units, and a warehouse with a sign over the door that read simply "Gear" which had a completely full parking lot. There were more of the inevitable drive-through espresso stands, one small grocery store with a liquor store attached, a sprawling Mormon church, and half a dozen bars, all with enormous parking lots. She passed two restaurants advertising fine dining on their signs, one old, one new, both with signs that read "Closed for the winter. See you next spring!"

She took a quick look down Gabe McGuire's driveway as she passed but didn't see anything. Stands of cottonwood marked where the creeks drained. Spruce in all flavors formed dark clumps everywhere you looked.

It was a very spread out community, she thought. As private as you wanted it to be, and evidently some liked it very private indeed. Given the real estate listings she and Liam had seen over the last six months they were willing to pay a high price for it and the taxes that came with it. She wondered what that charismatic Victorian reprobate, Albert Blewes, would have thought of his namesake. He would undoubtedly have become a realtor if he lived today.

She arrived back in town, braked at one of the four stoplights Blewestown boasted (Newenham still had none) and turned left to go down the hill. About halfway down she saw a person who could only be the infamous Sybilla Karlsen, because she was old, female, and naked. She pulled over to the shoulder and got out, slipping her jacket from her shoulders. "Hello," she said, smiling. "Are you Sybilla?"

The old lady, terribly thin with translucent skin and white hair standing up in a corona around her head, looked around. "Oh, hello," she said, beaming. "Who are you?"

"I'm Wyanet Chouinard," Wy said, slipping her jacket over Sybilla's shoulders. A pickup honked as it flashed by way too fast and Wy had just enough time to give the young man driving it a death glare before it was past. "But please call me Wy. You met my husband earlier this week. Liam? Liam Campbell?"

"Oh my yes," Sybilla said, allowing herself to be shepherded to the Forester and ensconced in the passenger seat. "What a nice young man. So handsome and so gentlemanly. He gave me a ride home."

"Yes, he told me. He enjoyed meeting you." Wy fastened Sybilla's seat belt.

Sybilla tutted. "I hate these infernal things. They clutch at you so." She smiled up at Wy. "I can think of more pleasant ways to be clutched."

Wy grinned. "So can I." She went around and got in. On impulse she said, "May I take you to lunch, Sybilla?"

Sybilla smiled beatifically. "Oh my yes, I'd love that—"

"Wy," Wy said. "Or Wyanet, if you like."

"What a lovely name."

"It's Lakota Sioux."

"And are you?"

"No." She hesitated, as Sybilla was of a generation that could find what she said next problematic. "I'm actually part Yupiq."

Sybilla looked delighted. "Really? Yupiq? We don't see many Yupiq in Southcentral. Sugpiaq, of course, some Tlingit, and a few Athabascan. But I don't remember meeting a Yupiq before now."

Wy thought of her maternal relatives in Icky. "Only half."

"Close enough for government work," Sybilla said firmly.

Wy laughed. "Let's stop by your place first and you can dress."

Sybilla looked down at Wy's jacket. "Oh my yes, this jacket certainly won't do for dining out."

What would do was a trim wool suit that looked very Jackie O., albeit it was now two sizes too large. Sybilla even had a pillbox hat to match that she anchored fiercely to her scant hair with two enormous bobby pins, and a pair of pumps dyed robin's egg blue to match the suit and hat which kept falling off because they were too big now, too. The attendant on duty, highly amused once Sybilla had been restored safely to her, advised Wy on places to eat and thus it was that Wy took Sybilla to the restaurant in the three-story hotel perched at the very end of the Spit, built entirely without fear of tsunami. The dining room was at the water's edge with real cloth napkins and tablecloths. Not bad for rural Alaska.

"I wonder if I'll ever get used to that view," Wy said. Seiners, drifters, pleasure craft, sailboats, a Coast Guard buoy tender, all passed in review on the other side of the window.

"I haven't and I've lived here for over thirty years, my dear," Sybilla said. The server appeared and she ordered a vodka martini with three olives and a steak sandwich, rare. Wy ordered a diet Coke and a bowl of clam chowder. The drinks came immediately—there was a lot to be said for eating out in the off season in a tourist town—and they toasted and sipped.

Sybilla, on her best society dame manners, said, "What do you do, dear?"

"I'm a pilot."

The martini, which was disappearing fast, paused midway. "You fly airplanes?"

"Yes."

Sybilla nodded her head at Wy's glass. "No consumption of alcohol within eight hours of flying."

"Yes."

"I will feel that much more safe when I fly with you, my dear. Do you work for an air taxi, or are you freelance?"

"Both, now, I guess. I owned my own air taxi in Newenham before we moved here. I'm basically on call for now." Only to the state of Alaska so far, but flight hours were billable hours no matter who she was in the air for.

"You owned your own business?" Something snapped together behind Sybilla's eyes and she became suddenly far more present. "What was your annual gross?"

Wy answered that and other questions about net income, expenses, insurance, depreciation, amortization, and taxes as best she could without her files in front of her. In the end Sybilla was pleased to give an approving nod. "Well done, my dear, well done, indeed. You sold it when you moved here, you said?"

"I did."

"Profitably, I hope."

Wy straightened in her chair. "Of course."

Sybilla signaled the waiter, addressed him by name, and ordered another martini. He looked at Wy and she shook her head. "Do you mean to start another business here in Blewestown?"

"I don't know," Wy said. "Not right away, at any rate."

"Thinking of starting a family, are you?"

It didn't matter what she said to this old lady, who would very probably forget it before lunch was over. Wy told her the truth. "No. I'm infertile."

Sybilla nodded. "I see. And how does your husband feel about that?"

"He says he's okay with it." As usual, whenever Wy thought about it, she wondered if it was true. "We have one son, adopted."

Sybilla's third martini arrived. Her hand was steady and her diction was perfect. Maybe octogenarian livers, having stood up under all their hosts could throw at them for that long, were impervious to further abuse. "I didn't have children, either, but in my case it was by choice. I had a good voice and a talent for business and, god knows, Alaska during the pipeline years was the place to make money. If you knew how, and I did. Customers would come in after nine weeks on the line, deposit an entire paycheck with the bartender, and drink until it was gone."

Wy had heard the stories. "Were they ever unhappy when they sobered up?"

Sybilla raised her eyebrows. "Some were, yes, but they were all over twenty-one. If they wanted to party in my club and they could afford to do so, I was happy to oblige."

Wy laughed. As she knew from long experience of the Bristol Bay fishery, there was no easier task than separating young men from their money. "And your husband?"

"I didn't meet Stanley until I was in my forties." Sybilla smiled at Wy over the rim of her glass, mischief in her eyes. "He came into Barney's one evening and never left."

"Love at first sight?"

"Every woman should have that experience at least once." Sybilla sighed reminiscently. "He was so handsome, my Stanley, and so very... determined." Her voice layered that last word with meaning. She smiled to herself and Wy could plainly see the vibrant, laughing ghost of the younger woman reflected in the older woman's eyes. "Much like your

Liam, I should think. Not the kind of men to take no for an answer." She quirked an eyebrow in Wy's direction. "I'm all for women's lib or whatever we are calling it nowadays, but oh my. There is something to be said for a man who wants what he wants and won't stop until he gets it."

"What happened to Stanley?"

"We had seven glorious years. And then he died. A drunk driver. At eight o'clock in the morning, can you imagine?" A sigh. "I sold the club and our house and moved to Blewestown."

"Why Blewestown?"

"Stanley designed and built the road here, for one thing. We spent a great deal of time here together. It was a way to remain close to him. And my brother lives here, and he's my only family, so I thought..."

"Is your brother still—here?" Wy said delicately.

Sybilla's mouth pulled down. "Oh yes, he's still here. Not that we see much of each other."

Not by Sybilla's choice, Wy deduced, and thought dark thoughts about the brother. Their food arrived, and it was hot and good if unremarkable and Wy was hungry. So was Sybilla, who had cleaned her plate as if she were eight instead of eighty. "What's for dessert, Wayne?" she said when the server returned.

He rattled off the selections and Sybilla chose the molten chocolate cake and Wy coffee with cream. Sybilla wanted to know what it was like, running an air taxi, and Wy beguiled her with stories of flying the mail to remote communities with airstrips like rock gardens and no flight service so dropping a half-used roll of toilet paper out the window to determine wind speed and direction was standard practice. Not to mention the inevitable curmudgeons who were annoyed that women, who had no business with their feet on the rudders in the first place, were entrusted with ferrying the You-Ess Mail. "That is to say, the ones who didn't propose marriage before I took off again."

Sybilla laughed delightedly. "How very flattering!"

"Not flattering at all. Golda Meir would have looked good to those guys."

"Oh my dear, the adventures you have had! How perfectly marvelous! Alaska has always been good at that, you know, at giving women an equal shot at whatever job was going. Mostly I think because there were so few people here to begin with, businesses were happy to hire anyone with a pulse. I had no trouble raising a loan to build my club." She winked at Wy. "Of course, it didn't hurt that the bank president had a reserved table down in front every Saturday night."

No, indeed.

Wayne brought the check and Sybilla gained her feet with some effort but her steps were perfectly steady on the way back to the car, even down the stairs in too-big shoes. Wy could only marvel. Three martinis would have put her on the floor and the next morning would not have been pretty. Sybilla's really was the Greatest Generation.

When they turned on Alder and drove past the trooper

post, they saw a young woman unlocking the door. "Oh, there's that nice young Petroff girl. Such a shame about her father. I wonder if she knew him?"

Evidently Sybilla's cognitive issue had kicked back in. Wy made a noncommittal murmur.

"Such a handsome young man, once he lost his puppy fat. All the girls after him, one could easily understand how it happened. Still, people can be so unkind. They were both in my class, you know."

Wy stopped at the stop sign. "What class?"

"Oh my dear, didn't I mention? I taught music and voice at the high school after I moved down here." She sighed. "So much tragedy for one family."

They pulled up in front of Sunset Heights, and the attendant, whom Wy now knew as Liz, came out to assist Sybilla from the Forester. It was high enough that it was a little matter of her swinging her legs over the side and sliding. She smoothed down her skirt and beamed at Wy. "What a lovely afternoon! What was your name again, dear?"

"Wy," Wy said. "Wyanet Chouinard."

"Wyanet, of course, dear. You'll come to tea one afternoon soon, won't you?"

"It would be my pleasure, Sybilla, thank you."

Liz made a signal for Wy to wait and ushered Sybilla inside. Wy was checking her phone when she emerged again to knock on the passenger side window. "Thank you," she said when Wy rolled down the window.

"What for?"

"First for the rescue and repatriation and then for the lunch."

"I enjoyed it."

"Come again, won't you? Most of our residents would be all the better for visits from friends and family."

"She's the first friend I've made in Blewestown," Wy said.

Liz smiled. "And now you have two."

"What's wrong with her? I know she's old, but—"

"Dementia," Liz said. "It manifests in forgetfulness, mostly."

Wy raised her eyebrows.

Liz sighed. "To the point that sometimes she goes walk-about before she gets dressed, yes, but so far she has always returned to the here and now. She's generally fairly cognizant and she is wonderfully healthy otherwise. It's easy for her to fool us into thinking she's fine, and then we turn our back for one minute and—" She snapped her fingers. "Some-times it's worse than keeping track of a two-year-old." She hesitated. "She's better when she has something to focus on. Like a visitor."

At least they weren't chaining Sybilla to her bed. "I'll be back often."

"Good." Liz stood back and waved her off.

Halfway to Sourdough her phone sounded the opening bars of "He's So Fine" and she pulled to the side of the street. "Hey."

"Hey, yourself. I need a ride."

"Where to?"

"Across the Bay. Kapilat."

Wy remembered the tiny community, half old, half new, perched on the edge of the fjord. "Usual rates?"

"Usual rates," he said grimly.

She didn't laugh. "Meet you at the tie-down."

Seventeen

Thursday, September 5

H E WAS STANDING NEXT TO THE CESSNA when she pulled up. "Hey," she said.

"Hey." He looked glum.

"I fueled up when I got back from Anchorage. Let me do the walk-around and we should be good to go."

He grunted. Monosyllabicy, if that was even a word, was his chosen means of communication when he was forced to fly.

She did the walk-around, noting that he'd already untied the lines and coiled them neatly next to their cleats. Poor Liam. He did what he could. "Okay, climb on in."

In the left seat she moved the yoke and the rudder pedals with her chin on her shoulder to check that the control surfaces were still working per spec. Next to her Liam buckled on his seatbelt and with both hands took a firm grip on his seat, preparatory to him helping her get and keep the aircraft in the air. Because she loved him she pretended she didn't notice.

Five minutes later they were in the air and following the Spit out into the Bay. He had yet to move a muscle.

"Hey," she said.

He sounded tense even over the headset. "Hey yourself."

"Did you feel like this when I took you up as my spotter during herring fishing?"

She couldn't see his eyes behind his sunglasses when his head turned but the tension in his jawline said it all. "Every second."

She was silenced for a moment. "God. I'm sorry, Liam."

"I'm an Alaskan. Worse, I'm an Alaska state trooper. What am I gonna do?"

The three islands guarding the entrance to a pair of narrow fjords slid beneath them before she spoke again. "If I'd known…"

"Can't be helped, Wy."

What was courage, again? Being terrified of something and doing it anyway? By that definition Liam Campbell had to be the bravest person she'd ever met. "What does it feel like?"

"What?"

"Being afraid to fly." She was genuinely curious, and a little ashamed that she had never asked him before. "Is it only mental or is it physical, or what?"

He thought about it, and out of the corner of her eye she noticed his grip relaxing on the edge of the seat. He didn't go so far as to let go but his knuckles were less white. "It starts with the physical. I get this, I don't know what to call it, this white flash up the back of my legs and up my spine when we lift off. It's debilitating, like I'm not sure if I could walk if I stood up. Or even if I could stand up."

"And you anticipate it."

"Yeah, which is what wrecks me even before I get on the damn plane. And no matter how many times I park my ass on a plane it never gets better." His sigh was heavy even over the headset. "I hate it."

"The feeling, not the flying?"

"Yeah. I mean, look at that." It was obvious it took an effort for him to turn his head to see out the window. "The best view in the world. Augustine and Iliamna and Redoubt. The Bay with all the boats carving those long, curving white wakes in it. Even on a cloudy day it's amazing, and it was just as amazing in Newenham, and it was when I flew into the Park to talk to Jim about Grant's murder." His shoulders raised in a slight shrug. "I know it's a privilege, this view, to see it. I know that. But…"

"You've always felt like this?"

"Always."

He didn't mention his father, the Air Force ace. He'd never said but she'd met the man and she could guess what his reaction would have been to his only son's fear of flying.

To distract him she embarked on the history of the town they were heading for. Kapilat had at one time been the big town on the Bay, home to five salmon canneries, a king crab processing plant, a hospital, a hotel, three bars, and four churches with actual resident pastors and priests. There had even at one time been a sit-down, popcorn-selling theater. It had been the main port of call for the Alaska Steamship Company in Southcentral Alaska. Everyone from all the other Bay settlements had perforce come to Kapilat to buy fuel and supplies, pick up their mail, and get their hair cut and their broken bones set. The Coast Guard had stationed a patrol boat there and some of their onshore housing was still standing. Kapilat had even sent the first woman to the territorial legislature, Harriet Browne, a pilot, in fact. She'd needed to be one, since there were only four voting districts in Alaska at the time and hers had stretched from Kenai to Adak to Cordova, resulting in her logging thousands of miles on her Stinson Reliant. Wy had found a photo of Browne standing in front of it on the Alaska Women's Hall of Fame website, and approved of Browne's choice of aircraft as she had no doubt that Browne would have taken advantage of constituent business trips by running freight on the side. Wy would have.

Even better from an admittedly Alaskan standpoint, Browne had married at least five times—"One way to secure a majority," Liam said—and her constituents had nicknamed her High Drift Factor Harry Browne, or High Drift Harry for short. She boasted that she had been excommunicated from the Pennsylvania Ministerium (Browne was originally from Pennsylvania), the Catholic Church (her third husband's religion), and the Church of Jesus Christ of Latter-day

Saints (her fourth's). That didn't seem to have lost her any votes, either, as she had been returned to office eight times and was still around to help lobby D.C. for statehood in the late fifties.

Wy descended to five hundred feet as unostentatiously as possible in the hope that Liam wouldn't notice, banked right to follow the bay east, and soon they were over the mouth of Mussel Bay. While the leaves on the deciduous trees had turned they still clung stubbornly to their branches, brilliant splashes of yellow and gold against the lush green backdrop of the evergreens that marched determinedly up the sides of the mountains, checked only by the snow and ice marching as determinedly down. Standoff. A dark red undergrowth formed picket lines between the warring factions, fireweed that had topped out and gone to seed and rusty leaves.

"Look," she said, and tipped the Cessna very slightly and very gently so he could look down at the water. He actually turned his head and even more miraculously kept his eyes open when he did. As if in reward, a late run of silvers jumped and splashed in the water below, powered by their own frantic need to return to spawn in the place of their birth. "Everything else followed those silvers into here," Wy said. "The Sugpiaq first; the Russians next, following the sea otters that followed the silvers; Western colonists after that; and *après ça, le déluge*. The Outside canneries, the white forefathers of the town of Kapilat, the ships of the Alaska Steamship Company, the US Postal Service, the US Coast Guard, the Blue Canoe."

"How big did it get?"

"I looked up the census numbers. In 1959, the year the US Congress passed the statehood act, Kapilat had a population of eight hundred. Doubled in the summer when all the Outside workers came to catch and can the salmon."

"Like Newenham."

She nodded. "Then in 1960, the Sterling Highway was built, 138 miles long, from Blewestown to Tern Lake, connecting the Seward Highway in mid-spate between Anchorage and Seward."

"The death knell."

"The first toll, maybe."

Once it became one of the few Alaskan towns with road access, Blewestown began to grow in population. Already in decline, the deciding blow for Kapilat came in March 1964 when the 9.2 Alaska Earthquake dropped Mussel Bay and Kapilat and the entire coast of Chungasqak Bay five and a half feet in elevation. The following April the moon and the sun lined up opposite each other with the earth in the middle and the spring tides washed up over the boardwalk that was Kapilat's main street. It cleaned out the first floors of the homes and businesses built alongside it, too. A year later the canneries had decamped for Kodiak or offshore in the form of floating processors that caught, flash froze, and transported everything direct to Adak or Dutch Harbor, there for air shipment Outside or internationally.

"The Japanese do love Alaskan fish," Liam said.

"Lucky for us." She banked left and flew halfway up the

bay to a salt-water slough with a bridge over it. Over the bridge the end of the strip appeared and she set down as gently as she could. The tension leached out of Liam as if someone had pulled a plug. He saw her noticing and he laughed, a short, relieved burst of sound. "At least no one shot a blade off the propeller that time."

"There's that," she said, grinning. Although the memory was no cause for humor. They could both have been killed. Lucky she'd had that hacksaw in her tool box.

They parked to one side of a large, empty hangar, and started to walk the dirt road into town. "Who are we going to see, again?"

"Alexei and Kimberley Petroff," he said. "They were at Gabe's party on Monday night. He's the chief of the local tribe and she's his wife."

"So, opportunity, and you say there are rocks all over the place so I guess there were means."

"For everyone."

"What about motive?"

"I don't know. Depends if Alexei is a tree cutter or not."

She knew what he meant. Some Alaska tribes wanted to exploit their resources; some wanted to protect what they had. In Alaska, no matter the community, it was always about what you could pull out of the ground and the water.

They walked up the dusty road to the bridge and crossed it into town. It was very small, one main street half a mile long paralleled by another small street and side streets connecting the two. It looked a lot like Blewestown's grid, on a smaller scale. "Paved, with curbs and sidewalks and even street signs," Wy said. "Just like downtown. I wonder who lives here with that kind of pull."

She could be forgiven her cynicism. It always came down to who lived where when it came to apportioning the state's budget. Sometimes Wy thought it would be more egalitarian to rotate legislative seats through all the villages, towns, and cities of the state on a regular basis. The pork might be sliced more thinly but at least everyone would get a piece. "Hey, there's a bar."

The Mussel Inn had a bar down the left and the inevitable old fart asleep with his head on it at one end. The right wall was lined with booths and the windows at the end overlooked the small boat harbor. It smelled strongly of deep fat frying and was lavishly festooned with fish nets decorated with corks, glass floats, and women's underwear. The woman behind the bar, a diminutive dyed blonde with a pierced lip, narrowed her eyes when they asked for directions to the Petroffs' home. "Why don't I call them to make sure they're home before you walk up?" she said, and didn't wait on their answer to do so. It was a brief conversation and she hung up and said, "Up Castner, turn left on Kiska, right on Traversie, and up the hill. They're at the top."

She didn't exactly hand them their hats but it was clear that if they weren't drinking they weren't welcome.

They followed her directions faithfully and came to Traversie and turned right. It was a short but steep climb.

They emerged at the top to find a solidly built two-story log house that had been there for a while but looked well cared for, logs oiled, roof freshly shingled, the frames of the many sash windows newly painted a bright white. A fenced garden and a shop big enough to hold a small drifter on a trailer could be seen behind the house.

As they approached the front door, it opened. Indubitably Alaska Native, Liam thought, medium/heavy with muscle, not fat, black/brown, early forties, no facial hair, no visible scars. Heavy brows that nearly met over his eyes in a permanent scowl. "Alexei Petroff?"

"You the trooper?"

"Yes. Liam Campbell. This is my wife and pilot, Wyanet Chouinard."

"I suppose this is about Erik." Petroff didn't wait for his answer, but stepped back, opening the door wide.

They went up the steps and inside. The door opened into a small entryway lined with boots and coats. They toed off their shoes, and Petroff led them into the living room, a corner room with windows on both sides. It was lined with Sheetrock painted white, making it a lot lighter than most cabins he had been in, and, he'd bet, a lot warmer in the winter. Just in case it wasn't, a rock fireplace with a metal insert and a fan had been built into a corner, and the furniture looked prebuilt and comfortable. "We'd like to speak to your wife, too, if she's home," Liam said.

There was movement in the doorway and they stepped back to get out of the way of a woman carrying a tray holding mugs and a carafe. "I thought you might like some coffee," she said. Also Alaska Native, medium/slight, black/brown, mid to late thirties. Her hair was pulled up and back with a clip and like all of them she wore a plaid shirt and jeans and socks on her feet. There were tiny gold hoops in her ears and a wedding ring on her left hand, no watch, but then who did wear watches anymore. She set the tray down on the coffee table and stood up, wiping her hands down her jeans, and looked at her husband.

"Please, sit," Petroff said, gesturing, and everyone sat down, Kimberley taking a chair opposite the couch instead of on it next to her husband. She sat on the very edge of the seat, her back straight with her hands clasped, until Petroff said, "You brought out the coffee, Kimberley, you might as well pour it."

"Oh." She poured out and handed mugs around with hands that might have been shaking a little.

"Is Sally Petroff any relation?" Liam said, hoping to ease the tension.

"Our daughter," Alexei said.

"She's my admin assistant at the post. A very capable young woman."

"Yes."

Okay. "So you've heard about Erik Berglund."

"I imagine everyone has by now," Alexei said. "No secrets on the Bay."

Kimberley turned her head to look out the window.

"It was not an accidental death," Liam said. "It appears

that the people at Gabe McGuire's party were the last to see him alive. I'm talking to everyone who attended to try to get a sense of how he spent his last hours."

Kimberley stood up. "I forgot the cream and sugar. I'll be right back."

Wy stood up and put her mug on the table. "May I help?" She followed Kimberley without waiting for an answer.

"Gabe invited us to see his new movie," Alexei said. "Food first, then a showing in his private theater. Dessert after, and then we went down to the boat and came home."

"It was pretty late when the party ended, after ten. Dark by then."

"It's only an hour trip." Alexei shrugged. "It was a clear night, and calm. Stars from horizon to horizon." First gleam of humanity.

"Did anyone see you come home?"

"Sergei Pete was on the slip when we pulled in. He caught my line, helped snug us down." He gave Liam Sergei's phone number.

"Did you talk to Erik Berglund that night?"

Alexei shrugged again. "Said hi, how you doing."

"Nothing about his work?"

"No."

A murmur of feminine voices, the words indistinguishable. "Erik Berglund showed me around his dig that day. He said he was trying to prove the existence of a traditional trail that led from the dig site to Soldotna and Kenai. He seemed to think it would affect exploratory drilling in the Bay."

Alexei snorted. "A broken snare and a couple of arrow-heads is not going to make any difference to the oil companies or to the state."

"He used to work for UNESCO. He seemed to think that they might step in."

Alexei rolled his eyes. "Yeah, yeah, we all heard how he wanted to turn the Bay into a World Heritage Site. Chungasqak Bay is not Mesa Verde. Besides, we don't need UNESCO coming in and telling us what our history is. We know what our history is."

He stopped when Kimberley reappeared. She set a creamer and a sugar bowl down on the tray and sat down, again on the very edge of her seat, eyes fixed on her clasped hands. Wy followed and sat down next to Liam.

"Forgive me, Ms. Petroff," Liam said, "but another guest said that he saw you in conversation with Mr. Berglund."

She clasped her hands again, but before she did he could see that they were in fact trembling. Her face was pale and she would not meet his eyes. "We went to high school in Blewestown together. We were just catching up."

"But the person who saw you said that your conversation looked intense. What were you—"

Alexei stood up. "That's enough. I'll see you out."

"Mr. Petroff—"

"We have nothing further to say to you, Sergeant. We're sorry Erik's dead but we don't know what happened to him. You've seen that so-called trail down to his so-called dig. Have you considered that he might have just fallen down it?"

Alexei stepped around the coffee table and perforce they stood up. By sheer force of presence Alexei shepherded them inexorably out of the living room, down the hall, and out the door.

As they came down the steps, two young men in their late teens pulled up in a pickup and hopped out. They were carbon copies of Alexei. "Hey, Mom." They looked curiously at Liam and Wy as they passed into the house. "You okay?"

Liam waited until they were on Traversie again before he spoke. "Kimberley say anything to you?"

"No, but she was trying very hard not to cry."

"I wish I'd been able to talk to her alone."

She looked at him. "You can make that happen."

"I know I can. And I may have to. I don't think Len Needham was lying when he said he saw them in conversation at the party. Or that they were arguing."

"Alexei didn't seem too pleased."

"No."

They walked in silence for a few moments. "You say everyone is telling you that Erik was quite the player. You think him and Kimberley—?"

"It would give Alexei quite the motive, wouldn't it?"

They walked down Traversie to where it intersected with Castner and kept going down Kiska toward the airport. They passed several more street signs, Buck, Kerdook, Pletnikoff. "Oh," Wy said. "That's it."

"What's it?"

She was smiling. "I told you about Kapilat, right? It got wiped out by the tidal wave in the '64 quake and the high tides after the land dropped?"

"Yes?"

"They bulldozed what was left and rebuilt the town the way we see it here today. That's why the houses look so new. The Petroffs' house is probably the oldest one in town because it was so high up it didn't get hit."

"Okay?"

"The two main streets are named Attu and Kiska." She pointed at the nearest sign. "And the cross streets are named from the roster of the Alaska Scouts. One of them must have lived here, or, I don't know, been a child of."

"Oh. Oh yeah. Okay, all right, pretty cool spotting there, Ms. Chouinard."

"Pretty cool doing," she said. "I like this town."

When they walked past the cell tower sitting off Kerdook he called Sergei Pete, who was pleased to pick up on the first ring and confirm Alexei and Kimberley Petroff's alibi in every detail. "So much for that possibility," Liam said. "Motive, maybe, but no opportunity."

"The good news is your list is shrinking."

"It wasn't that big to begin with." And he had to get back on the plane.

Wy's phone rang as they arrived at the airstrip, Prince all over it with "Sexy MF." Wy looked up to see Liam smirking at her. She rolled her eyes and showed him the screen. It was Tim. "Hey," she said. "How's my guy?"

"Is that Liam I hear laughing?" Tim said.

His voice sounded deeper and more confident than the last time she'd spoken to him, although that might be her imagination. The boy hiding from his birth mother under the porch of their shack in Ualik was a distant memory. Or so she hoped. "Ignore him. How are you?"

"Are you in Blewestown yet?"

"Got here Monday. Gorgeous weather, I could have been here in time for lunch, but I took the scenic route."

"The new house okay?"

"Yeah. Unbelievably it's as nice as advertised, and we've already had our first house guest."

"I bet that'd be the one, the only Jo Dunaway."

"You'd win that bet."

"So annoying," he said. "I wanted to be your first guest."

"You can be our second," she said, trying not to sound too needy.

"She stopped by to say hi on her way down."

"She said. Said you looked like you were doing good."

"Yeah," he said. "I was thinking of driving down next weekend. Or, no, the weekend after that, I've got a big ass test coming up the Monday after next weekend." He hesitated. "Okay if I bring someone with me?"

Liam saw Wy come to attention. "A guest would be fine," she said, elaborately casual. "Anybody we know?" He mumbled something. "I'm sorry, what?"

"It's a friend," he said at better volume, and this time she could clearly hear the embarrassment.

"What's her name?" Liam's eyes widened and he made a jerk-off motion with his hand. She pretended she didn't see.

"I didn't say she was a girl."

"You just did."

He grumbled. "You think you're so smart."

"What's her name and where is she from?"

"Anna Barnes. She's from Cordova. She's studying for an A&P certificate, too."

"Well, tell Anna we'd be happy to have her come visit," Wy said, trying not to purr. "Will you require one room or two?"

"Mom!"

"Hey, just being a good hostess." She dropped the teasing note. "Can't wait to see you, kid. I love you."

"Yeah, yeah. I'll text when we leave."

"Okay." She clicked off and beamed at Liam. "He's coming and he's bringing a girl with him."

"I heard. I'm glad the guest bedrooms are on the other side of the house."

"Liam!"

They taxied up to the tie-down in Blewestown twenty minutes later. Liam's phone rang as he got out (Britney Spears and "I'm a Slave 4 U"). It was Hans Brilleaux, the medical examiner, in Anchorage. He was just glad it wasn't Barton. "Hey, Brillo," he said.

"WHAT KIND OF CRAZY FUCKING ASSHOLE DOES THIS, CAMPBELL?"

Liam yanked the phone away from his ear. "Jesus, Brillo. Dial it down, wouldya? I've only got two eardrums and Barton's already taken out one."

There was a heavy exhale. When Brillo spoke again he had dialed it down but Liam could hear the hard edge of rage as plain as if Brillo was in his face like the wire-haired terrier he was, teeth bared and sharp enough to draw blood. "I want to know what kind of sick, sorry, sadist does this kind of thing. And then I want you to shoot them."

"What kind of thing? Is this about Erik Berglund?"

A silence, where Liam got the impression that Brillo was working at containing his anger and not succeeding very well. "No," he said very precisely. "It is not about Erik Berglund. It's about the skeleton you dropped on me along with Erik Berglund.

"All of his long bones are broken in multiple places, humerus, ulna, radius, femur, tib/fib. The feet were broken at the joints. The spine half a dozen times. And the skull... Jesus, Liam. It's like someone tried to pulverize it."

"His?" Liam said.

"It's a boy. I'd say about ten years old."

"How long has the body been there?"

"Thirty years, give or take."

"Jesus."

He thought about the cave behind the cave and the limited access between them. And then he realized what must have happened. Someone had deliberately broken the bones of the body of the ten-year-old boy into pieces small enough to fit through the crack, which was so narrow no one would ever find it, or if they did, think to look for anything inside it.

Except maybe another ten-year-old kid. It was why the bones were so close to the crack, he realized. The killer couldn't shove them in any farther because the crack was so narrow. He hadn't been able to get his arm in past his bicep. "Brillo, can you tell if the injuries were pre- or post-mortem?"

"I'm pretty sure the fracture on the left side of the skull was the killing blow. If he wasn't dead he would have been unconscious or comatose when the rest of his body was broken into bits and pieces. Do you know who did it, Liam?"

"Not yet."

"Find him."

This wasn't professional, Brillo's rage, it was personal. Child killings brought out the vengeful god in everyone. "What about Erik Berglund?"

He heard keys clicking. "Oddly enough, Berglund's injuries were similar if not as extensive. There was a blow to the left side of his head, and his left elbow and clavicle are cracked. He's also got a hell of a lot of cuts and bruises, and his hands are all torn up. Was there blood at the scene?"

"Not a lot, no."

"Could he have fallen after he was struck?"

Liam thought of that sidewinder of a trail leading to the dig. Erik could have been struck at the signpost. "Yes."

And then fallen all the way down it, and at the bottom crawled to the tent and into the cave. And he had then tried to make a call on his dead phone.

He remembered the wear and tear on Erik's clothes. Liam hadn't looked closely at the trail but he had looked. It had rained on Tuesday and the body hadn't been found until Wednesday. The rain must have washed away any blood. "Time of death?"

"How cold is it in that cave?"

"Say fifty degrees or thereabouts."

Brillo grunted. "Then I'd say somewhere between Monday night and Tuesday morning."

What Liam had estimated. "Okay. Thanks, Brillo."

"Find that fucker, Campbell."

"I will."

Liam clicked off and thought bleakly of the new scenario laying itself out before him. If Erik had been attacked at the top of the trail and not the bottom, then anyone of any size or age could have done it without negotiating that killer trail. His pool of potential suspects had grown to include anyone in the general area of the Lower Peninsula on Monday night.

Great.

Eighteen

Friday, September 6

THE NEXT MORNING LIAM WENT STRAIGHT to the post, told his administrative aide that he wasn't in to anyone who called, and locked himself in his office.

He took a ruler, a pencil, and a blank piece of paper and created a grid. In the central square he wrote "Erik Berglund." He got out his phone and opened the Notes app and began filling in the squares around Berglund.

Gabe McGuire. Lived almost on top of Erik's dig. By his own admission had a beef with Berglund over the right of way, but Liam was no scalp hunter and with the best will in the world he couldn't put McGuire in the frame. He had more to lose than all of the other suspects put together. He had motive and he sure had opportunity, though, so McGuire went in a square next to Erik.

Leonard Needham. Liam had googled him. The list of hits went on for fourteen pages, with some stunt nerds doing—or trying to—YouTube recreations of some of his more famous stunts. The one where he'd jumped from a moving car into a moving plane and then parachuted out of the plane onto the top of a moving semi was among Liam's least favorites.

He shook his head. Someone who had had his ten best stunts written up in *Popular Mechanics* with color commentary by a physicist and a mechanical engineer was not likely to orchestrate something as clumsy as murder by blunt instrument and cliff. Further, Needham had advised his nephew to fess up about vacating the right of way. A straight arrow, or wanting to appear like one. Needham wasn't entirely out of the running, either, but he got a square on the outer edge of the grid.

The Kinnisons and the Reeses both got squares on the outer edge. A cursory troll through state databases showed him that Cynthia Reese was a realtor and her husband owned the go-to local marine supply store. Greg Kinnison was a physical therapist and his wife Grace a dentist. Their only stake here was the ability to brag about being friends with Gabe McGuire. Although they probably wouldn't object to gating the community, either.

What the hell was it with people who, so long as they had theirs, were no longer willing to share? By law beaches in Alaska were public up to the high water mark but it meant nothing to the general population if there was no access to them. Like Alaska's national parks and wildlife refuges. You could drive into Denali, you could even drive to the Gates of the Arctic, but Wood-Tikchik and too many others required air transportation, which was never cheap and so out of the reach of most citizens.

Domenica Garland. She was one of McGuire's nearest neighbors, so opportunity. If Brillo was right, and he usually was, anyone had means. Motive? Plenty, in this case, ranging from the professional to the personal. Personally, she and Berglund had been fuck buddies. She acted like it didn't matter that it had ended but who the hell knew with women? Professionally, she wanted to drill for oil in the Bay, and Berglund was about to begin a study that might not stop the drilling but it wouldn't hurry it along, either, especially if Berglund managed to get an entity as high profile as UNESCO involved. Erik had been a good-looking guy and Liam could see her sleeping with him as an exercise in vanity, but killing him over what had appeared to Liam to be a pretty pitiful collection of artifacts seemed extreme, especially in a state with a legislature which regarded the resource extraction industry as a cash cow. God knows the industry had bought enough members of that body their seats. Liam didn't think Garland regarded Erik Berglund as even the mildest threat to her job or her plans to drill for oil and gas in the Bay. Still, she had more motive than most, so she went into a square next to Erik.

Jeff and Marcy Ninkasi, friendly with everyone, sold beer to everyone, and still would if UNESCO declared the entire lower Kenai a World Heritage Site or RPetCo turned the Bay into the next North Slope. Didn't live in the neighborhood so no stake in the right of way controversy. Outer edge.

Hilary Houten. Rival archeologist. Liam had seen the dislike between the two of them at Backdraft and the Chamber
and heard of it at the party. Houten had forty years on
Berglund and Berglund had at least a hundred pounds on
Houten. Brillo said Berglund had been struck hard on the
side of the head and that the rest of his injuries might have
come afterward. Liam couldn't imagine a scenario involving
a physical confrontation between the two, certainly not one
that ended with Berglund dead. But professional jealousy
was a powerful motivator. He put Houten's name on a square
next to Berglund's.

Aiden Donohoe and wife Shirley. Classic Alaska Boomer.
Dismissive of Berglund's alleged discoveries. Didn't live in
the neighborhood but would undoubtedly want to cater to
Blewestown's most famous citizen. If Blue Jay Jefferson had
just donated fifty large to the Chamber to spur development
along, what fantastic sum could be hoped for from Gabe
McGuire? That would be worth at least one phone call to the
borough in support of vacating the right of way. Wouldn't
hurt Donohoe's feelings any to see Berglund and his touchy-
feely notions of preserving the Bay for all posterity dead and
gone, but he wouldn't at all like a murder tarnishing the
rep of his perfect little community by the sea, either. Outer
edge, with Shirley, who ran a local beauty salon.

And speaking of Blue Jay Jefferson. Another quintessential
Alaskan old fart, like Moses Alakuyak, yet not at all like that
obstreperous old timer. For one thing Jefferson was white
and Moses had been Yupiq, and although Moses would

have repudiated the notion in incendiary language a gulf of privilege would have separated the two. According to Ms. Petroff, Blue Jay Jefferson was a boomer, a charter member of the Spit and Argue Club, a former state legislator, chair of (pick one) the Alcohol Beverage Control board, the Alaska Industrial Development and Economic Authority, and the state Republican Party. In his day he'd been a lobbyist for every oil company who'd punched a hole anywhere in the state. He'd been set to run for governor until he came out against the PFD and it was too much to ask Alaskans to vote for someone who wanted to sideline their gravy train. Boomers like Jefferson and Donohoe regarded any economic activity as good economic activity. Pissed at Berglund for holding that up, but again, another creaky old guy who barely had enough strength to stand up on his own two legs. Outer edge.

Alexei and Kimberley Petroff went right into separate boxes next to Berglund before Liam even thought about it, based on nothing but his interview with them the day before. There was something there, he just didn't know what. Yet.

He raised his head and looked at the door that led to the outer office. Ms. Petroff was obeying his orders to leave him strictly alone this morning. No. Nope. Not. The sins of the father and all that. Absolutely no reason to add her name to the grid.

Allison Levy, Jake Hansen, and Paula Pederson, along with Hansen's wife, Lily, went on the outer edge. The first three were members of the Blewestown City Council. The Hansens ran a halibut charter during the summer and fished commercially during the winter. Allison Levy ran a bed-and-breakfast and Paula Pederson grew peonies in commercial quantities and FedExed them to brides all over the South 48. So far as Liam could tell the four of them were there to round out the group of local movers and shakers slash neighbors, all of whom, if McGuire stroked them enough, might help him block off the road to the beach. He reached all of them by phone. All of them told the same story, bed before midnight.

He tossed down his pencil with an exasperated sigh and sat back in his chair to look at the map of Blewestown and environs that Ms. Petroff had produced in record time. If it didn't fill quite all of the wall it covered a decent portion of it. The bar scale showed 1 inch : 1 mile. He got up and went over to stand in front of it. He found Heavenly Drive and traced it with his forefinger to Augustine Lane, their street, and drew a small red heart, a smile pulling up the corner of his mouth.

He found Baranov Avenue and penciled an X next to the junk yard. He'd looked up the owner in the borough's parcel viewer and run them through the state records. The guy had been inside for everything from disturbing the peace to felony distribution, but the state hadn't managed to keep him there for more than a year at a time.

And the place didn't feel like the headquarters of the drug organization Barton alleged to exist. A professional dealer would know not to draw attention his or her way, and certainly not by stockpiling junk all over their property.

A professional dealer would find a house on a busy but respectable street where the traffic in and out wouldn't draw attention. No, this guy was an individual entrepreneur.

He called Chief Rafferty and suggested she take in the sights along Baranov Avenue. She said she'd be delighted.

He looked back at the map. The rocky outcropping that formed what Erik Berglund had believed to be a rough natural dock was barely a smudge. He drew a shovel to mark the spot.

He went back to his desk and sat down with his hands behind his head, staring at the map. It had contour lines on land and depth contours on water. The darker the green on land, the higher the elevation, and the darker the blue at sea, the deeper the water. The coves, bays and inlets on the south side of the Bay were lapis lazuli, while the north side of the Bay, the Blewestown side, was such a pale blue as to be almost gray where it was nearest to shore. It was all sand, all the way down from Wolverine River at the head of the bay to the Spit, around Cook's Point and north all the way up to Turnagain. There was coal in the bluff that fronted the beach that had been mined for steamship fuel back in the day, and offshore platforms producing oil and natural gas lined the western side of Cook Inlet. Liam was no expert but it followed that sooner or later RPetCo or someone else would start punching holes in the Bay to see what was there. Where there was promise of a valuable resource in quantity, someone always did. It was the history of Alaska, beginning with the Russians and the sea otters.

He needed to find Erik's cabin. It was reasonable to expect that it was somewhere out East Bay Road because that's where the dig was and who liked a long commute? Except Judge DeWinter. He had emptied Erik's pockets and found keys only to Erik's truck. From what he had heard so far about dry cabins it might not have a lock. Or even a door.

On impulse, he picked up his cell, opened his contacts, and tapped on one. The contact picked up after the first ring. "How you doing, Dumbledore?" he said.

"Fuck off, Campbell."

Something inside him relaxed at the sound of that deep, assured voice. "Hey, Jim. Where are you?"

"In the Park. At home." There was a woman's voice in the background. "It's Liam."

"Is that Kate? Tell her I said hey."

"Liam says hey. Kate says hey back, and are you calling from Newenham?"

"From Blewestown, actually. On Chungasqak Bay."

Liam heard what he assumed was coffee pouring, followed by a slurp. "Never been there, but I hear it's scenic."

"It is that."

"You and Wy there on vacation?"

"No. They opened a post here and Barton asked me to take it on."

"Huh. I thought he was pretty happy with you in Newenham."

Liam sighed. "I think he's trying to move me closer to Anchorage."

"He did." Jim's voice had a smile in it. "Was a time you'd have been happy about that."

"That was then, this is now. I made it back up to sergeant, that's good enough. I don't want to deal with the politics. Hey, you get that school of yours up and running?"

"It's up, I don't know how well it's running."

"Pretty cool, though."

"If I can make it go how I want to, yeah."

"I hear Kate finally took down Erland Bannister."

"Well, he died on her before she could put him back in jail, but yeah. We're all good here, Liam. Why are you in Blewestown?"

"Barton says the drug trade has moved into the lower Kenai hard, manufacturing and distribution. He wants me to clean it up, like we did in the Valley."

"He wants to ride you into headquarters on a wave of trophy shots."

"I think so."

A brief silence. "And?"

Liam shook his head. "And I haven't been here a week and the local PD chief schooled me on exactly and precisely where I'm allowed to serve and protect, and the local judge warned me off using excessive force. Plus I got a dead archeologist, murdered last Monday night or thereabouts, and the skeleton of a ten-year-old boy, also murdered, that Brillo says has been lying where I found it for thirty plus years."

A brief silence. "Anything else?"

"The whole place feels off. I think it's partly because

Blewestown is the whitest town I've ever been in in Alaska. Everybody's white here, Jim. Except for my administrative aide. Whom Barton hired before I even got here, FYI."

"Yeah, she's probably spying on you for him."

"Be my guess. The only other Natives I've met are her parents who, I'm overjoyed to relate, are involved in my murder case, and I had to get Wy to fly me across the Bay to meet them. Newenham was majority Yupiq. It looked like Alaska. This place looks like, I don't know. Idaho. You know. If Idaho wasn't landlocked."

"How is Wy?"

"Fine. She sold her air taxi in Newenham. She's figuring out what she wants to do next."

"She keep both planes?" A pilot's question.

"Yeah. She meant to sell the Cub but when it came right down to it she couldn't."

"Don't blame her. Got a place to live?" Jim had thoroughly enjoyed the story of Liam's Progress through Newenham housing.

"Yeah, a nice one. Local guy built it for his wife and two kids. Kids are gone and he opened a brewpub in town and moved in over the shop. For sale by owner, saved us a ton of money. Got a hell of a view. I can't get too close to the edge of the yard because we're right on the bluff that backs up the town and it is seriously all downhill from there."

Another slurp. "How far away are you from retirement?"

"Two years."

"You can always pull the plug. I haven't looked back."

"I've thought about it," Liam said. "The thing is, I don't know what the hell else I'd do if I did. All I know is I don't want to live in Anchorage, and I sure as hell don't want any job that involves interacting with the goddamn legislature."

"You can always say no."

"You've met John Barton, right?"

A laugh. "Yeah. Still. You're a grown ass man, Liam. Figure out what you want and make your own damn decisions."

If only I knew what that was, Liam thought after he'd said goodbye and hung up.

Nineteen

Friday, September 6

WY SPENT THE MORNING UNPACKING, and then made a trip to the grocery store. There were two in Blewestown and neither of them was AC, a nice change from Newenham, where, like almost everywhere else in Alaska that was not on the road system, the Alaska Commercial Company had a lock on the sale of groceries.

It amused her to stand in line and eavesdrop. The cashiers seemed to know all the customers, the customers appeared to be all local all the time, and they were united in their joy at the end of tourist season and the beginning of the school year. She was picking up the local vernacular, too. For starters, almost none of the locals called Blewestown "Blewestown". It was the Bay, or Baytown, or B-town, or, sometimes, Chungasqak. This last was employed with the emphasis that Alaskans in general used in calling Denali Denali and never McKinley, an Outsider who'd never even been to the state. She resolved to look up the meaning of "chungasqak" as soon as she got home, and Kapilat, Engaqutaq, and Chuwawet while she was at it. There was no one here to discourage her from learning the local Native language, so why not?

In even more thrilling news, there was also an honest-to-god bookstore—she parked in front and peered into the windows to be sure—and she took careful note of their hours. The last time she'd lived in a town with a bookstore she'd been in college.

When she got home she did another round of form on the deck just because she could. The deck here had fewer nail pops and warped boards and so was less prone to trip her up during Fair Ladies Work at Shuttle. She showered and dressed, and thought about going down to Blue Sky Air and introducing herself. She felt strangely reluctant to do so, and wondered at herself.

Maybe it was that she'd never had a vacation before. Her adoptive parents had been very strict about earning one's way in life and she'd been brought up to work. In college she'd always had full time jobs between semesters, and after she'd started Nushugak Air she was determined never to turn down a job. Summers were naturally her busiest season, what with flying fishermen and processor workers back and forth, the occasional flightseeing charter, and that one year she herring spotted for that asshole Cecil Wolfe. But fall kept her hopping, too, hauling hunters into and out of their camps and lodges. Winter, although the dark reduced flying hours, still saw an increase in local travel, school trips, shopping trips, basketball games, any distraction to hold off cabin fever. It was great for business, especially since in her Cub she could get into and out of the most rudimentary strips. It made hers the go-to flight service for a lot of folks between Newenham and Togiak, which was what she'd been aiming for, and helped her pay off both aircraft in record time, another goal. Wy hated owing money.

And regular customers could be very unforgiving. If you missed a pickup or a drop-off, it didn't matter if you had a perfectly valid excuse, like a hundred year storm blowing in off the Bering, or someone else pranging their plane at the Newenham airport and halting all air traffic for hours. If someone in Port of Call missed their Alaska Airlines flight in Newenham because you didn't pick them up on time, you could kiss that customer and all their future revenue goodbye.

Put it all together and owning and operating an air taxi made the prospect of time off a joke. This was a new experience for her and she didn't know quite what to do with herself.

Fortuitously, at just that moment the phone rang. It was Liz at Sunset Heights. "Sybilla wanted me to call to make sure you were coming to lunch today. Noon."

"I thought that was tea on Sunday." Wy could almost hear Liz shrug. "Tell her I'll be there."

It was an hour until noon and she decided to drive down to the airport and check on her aircraft. Both were snug at their tie-downs, and she took the time to give them a critical once-over. After the trip from Newenham the Cub was coming up on its annual inspection. The Cessna had another six months to go. It was time to replace the headsets and both could use new paint.

She saw someone working on the engine of a red and silver Beaver in front of a large empty hangar and walked over to introduce herself. She'd had her fill of shoveling snow off two sets of wings, and if she could find someone to paint her planes she'd need a place out of the weather for the paint to cure.

The mechanic, skinny, white, in his thirties, wearing Carhartt bibs he might have inherited from his grandfather, gave her the hangar owner's contact info. She tapped it into her phone.

Watching her, he said, "Would you like to meet me for a beer sometime?"

She flashed her wedding ring. "Married." She smiled at him to make sure that he understood the implied "if only" in her refusal. "Sorry."

His grin was gap-toothed and charming. "Worth a try."

She laughed and went back to her Forester with maybe just a little swash to her buckle and drove to Sunset Heights. Sybilla was already seated at a table in a small cafeteria that smelled strongly of Clorox and overcooked pasta. No cloth napkins here, but they did have table service in the form of a smiling teenager dressed in a blue and white striped apron. "Fried salmon steaks and a tossed salad today, Mrs. Karlsen." She smiled at Wy. "Can I get you ladies something to drink?"

"Water is fine for me," Wy said.

"Vodka martini, three olives," Sybilla said.

"Coming right up, Mrs. Karlsen." She reappeared in a moment with tall glasses of ice water and a small pitcher for refills.

"So nice that you could join me for lunch today, dear," Sybilla said.

"If you hadn't called I'd be eating a PBJ standing over the sink."

Sybilla chuckled. "My good deed for the day."

The salmon when it came was not overcooked, an almost impossible feat in an institutional setting. Wy was impressed, and laid in with a will.

"How is your young man settling in?" Sybilla said.

"He's at work on a case."

Again she saw that kind of click at the back of Sybilla's eyes, where in an instant she seemed to be tracking everything said to her. "He has a case?"

"He does." Wy hesitated.

Sybilla sniffed. "Afraid to upset the old lady, Wy? Is it Erik?"

Wy paused with her fork halfway to her mouth.

This time Sybilla snorted. "I thought you said you came from a small town." She sighed. "I warned him."

It took a moment for her words to register. "I beg your pardon? You warned Liam?"

Sybilla huffed an impatient sigh. "Not Liam. I warned Erik, when he came here to ask if he could rent my cabin."

"Erik? Erik Berglund?"

Sybilla looked annoyed. "Of course, Erik Berglund. Unless someone else has been murdered this week I don't know about. In which case your young man would certainly have been posted to the right place."

Wy put down her folk and said brightly, "Sybilla, why don't I call Liam and see if he can join us for dessert?"

Dessert was ice cream sundaes. Liam's melted in front of him as he asked questions and Sybilla answered them between bites.

Liam was, to put it mildly, chagrined. He'd asked everyone he had met in Blewestown if they knew where Erik Berglund lived, except for Sybilla. The one person he could be said to have spent more time with than the rest of them put together, and the one with more institutional memory of the place than anyone else save Jefferson and Houten. Seeing her marching down the street in the altogether had inclined him to dismiss anything she said. It was an epic fail on his part. "Where exactly is your cabin, Sybilla?"

"At the end of Crow's Nest."

Liam nodded. "And where is Crow's Nest?"

Sybilla had to get on the outside of a heaping spoonful of sundae before she could answer. Age had certainly not interfered with her appetite. "It's off Backstay, which is off Telltale." She saw his expression and relented. "It's in the

Full Sail Subdivision, about five miles out East Bay Road. The developer was a sailor."

"Who knew?" Wy said.

He already had his phone out and Wy could see he had called up Google Maps. "Where on Crow's Nest, Sybilla? What's the street address?"

She scraped her bowl with the spoon. "It's the last cabin at the end of Crow's Nest. Way up high, far away from anyone else." Her smile was dreamy. "Stanley and I spent as much time there as we could spare from our jobs. Our aerie, we called it."

Liam pocketed his phone. "Well, thanks, Sybilla—"

Wy touched his arm and he looked at her. "Sybilla," she said, "you said you had warned Erik, when he came to ask you if he could rent your cabin."

Sybilla licked her spoon and set it and the bowl aside with regret. "Yes, I did. Erik was one of my students. Well, both of them were." She sighed. "That's the best age, ten, when everything is bright and shiny and new, when nothing is impossible, when they'll believe anything you tell them without question, learn everything you have to offer and beg for more. Josh and Erik were inseparable." She folded her hands in front of her and stared into the past.

Liam would have said something, but again, Wy touched his arm. She waited long enough for the question to be only inquiring, not interrogational, and kept her tone gentle. "Who was Josh, Sybilla?"

Sybilla blinked at her. "Josh? Didn't I say? Joshua Petroff.

He was Erik's best friend." She shook her head. "I never believed all that rubbish they said about Erik afterward. He was attacked and left for dead. It was ridiculous to insinuate that he was faking his amnesia. People can be so cruel, and to say such things of a ten-year-old boy was unconscionable." Her eyes flashed. "And I said so at the time."

Liam had his phone out again and was doing another search. Wy guessed it was of Joshua Petroff. When he went rigid beside her, she was sure of it. "Why did you warn Erik, Sybilla?" she said.

"Warn Erik?" Sybilla looked bewildered. "Whatever are you talking about, my dear? Erik who?"

As they got up to leave Wy thanked Sybilla for lunch and Sybilla said brightly, "Don't forget tea on Sunday." She gave Liam an up-from-under look. "And bring your nice young man with you."

He surprised her by stooping to kiss her cheek. "I wouldn't miss it, Sybilla."

She blushed and smiled.

Outside, Wy said, "Can I come with you to check out the cabin?" She wanted to see what an aerie looked like.

Liam stood with his hands on his hips, frowning at his feet. She recognized the signs and waited. It was a good five minutes before he looked up again. "Ride with me."

"Okay." She climbed into his pickup and was surprised when they got to Sourdough that he didn't turn left to head out East Bay Road. Instead he continued down Alder to the post.

He pulled in and killed the engine. "Come inside with me and follow my lead."

"Okay?"

Ms. Petroff was at her desk, looking every bit as terrifyingly poised as Liam had described. "Ms. Petroff, this is my wife, Wyanet Chouinard."

"How do you do, Ms. Chouinard."

Wy bit back a smile and said gravely, "Ms. Petroff."

Liam led the way to his office. He had left the door open. Wy felt her amusement fade when she understood what that meant.

He stood in front of the map that covered half of one wall. "What did Sybilla say, Wy?" he said in a voice pitched to carry. "About five miles out East Bay Road?"

"Yes," she said, at a matching volume. "And all the streets were named for sailboat parts or something weird like that."

"Let's see if we can find it on this map." He poked his head out the door. "Ms. Petroff? Do you have a ruler I could borrow?" Wy closed her eyes and shook her head. Subtle Liam was not.

"Of course, sir." Did Ms. Petroff's voice sound a little higher? A drawer opened and closed, followed by footsteps.

"Thanks." He ducked back into the office. He wasn't smiling. Wy took the ruler and held it against the bar scale and then against the road. "That's about five miles."

They brought their faces close to the map. "There?"

Wy pushed his finger away. "No, there."

Mainsail Drive was a left turn off East Bay Road and if

the elevation contours were accurate, climbed nine hundred feet in a series of twists and turns to end just beneath the bluff that held up the road their own house was on, Heavenly View Drive. There were many streets in the subdivision but the scale wasn't large enough to include their names.

Wy looked at Liam, eyebrows raised.

He stepped back from the map, still speaking in that unnaturally loud voice. "Damn it, I've got that interview with Garfield at three o'clock and it's going to be a long one. I can't get out there and back in time. I'll have to wait until afterward."

Garfield? Wy mouthed at him, and he made a come-along motion with his hand.

"I've got some errands to run," she said obediently. "Why don't we meet up at home and drive out after dinner?"

She was rewarded by an approving nod. "That sounds great, I'll see you then."

"Okay." She took a step back, only to be snatched up in his arms and thoroughly kissed, just long enough for things to get interesting before he let her go again. Her hair had come loose from its braid and fallen into her eyes and she frowned at him while she tried to tuck it away again with shaking hands.

He noticed and grinned.

She stuck her nose in the air and left with as much flounce as she could muster on shaky knees. "Ms. Petroff," she said as she passed the aide's desk.

"Ms. Chouinard."

In the fleeting glimpse Wy had of her, she saw that the aide's professional mask had slipped a little.

She looked, Wy thought, afraid.

Liam didn't close his door as that might have given the game away. He sat down at his desk and pulled open the central drawer where he'd put the file folder containing the square and his notes on the list of suspects. He stopped himself from picking it up at the last moment.

He couldn't be sure but he thought it wasn't in the same place he had left it. It was farther back in the drawer now, exposing the pencil tray.

He raised his head and looked in the direction of the front office. If he had had any doubts, they were gone now.

🦌

Wy was waiting at the door when he drove up and she hustled down the steps and into the truck. She was carrying a paper bag. "I made you a sandwich," she said. "What did she do?"

He investigated the bag. Tuna with mayo, onions, and sweet pickles on white, his favorite.

She handed him a thermos. "Coffee."

"I love you."

"I know. Now give."

"She stayed at her desk all afternoon," he said around his first bite. He put the Silverado in gear and backed out of the drive one-handed and turned right on Heavenly Drive.

"You were there, too? What about your fake appointment?"

"I turned up the volume so she could hear it and hit the ringtone on my phone, which I pretended to answer and pretended to be disappointed that my fake meeting had been cancelled." He looked at her. "'F*ck and Run,' Wy? Really?"

"What?" she said, making with the big eyes. "Who doesn't love Liz Phair?"

"Maybe a little NSFW with the ringtones, is all I'm saying."

"You should talk." She made a strategic change of subject. "You don't really think Ms. Petroff killed Erik Berglund, do you?"

He glanced at her before turning right on Alder. "Anybody can kill anybody, Wy. As you well know."

"But—"

"Did you follow the link I sent you?"

"Yes."

"So you know that thirty years ago her father's brother and Erik's best bud disappeared off the same stretch of beach that Erik's dig fronted. Erik was found unconscious from a knock on the head. Due to retrograde amnesia he never regained his memories of that day."

"Yes."

"She would have known the story from her family. I think when Erik showed back up in the Bay that she would have wanted to talk to him. But she didn't mention that." He stopped at Sourdough at the bottom of the hill and turned left, crossing Spit where it became East Bay. He pushed the trip meter until it registered zero and continued down the road. "Her parents know something, too. You were there, you saw their reactions to Berglund's death."

Wy thought of Kimberley, weeping silently over the sink in her kitchen. "I don't know, Liam. I think there might be something else going on there."

"She lied to me about knowing where Erik was living," he said flatly.

Liam could forgive a lot, but seldom a lie. And he had liked young Ms. Petroff, so the betrayal stung all the more. And he had liked Erik Berglund, too, which only added to his determination to find out what had happened to him. "Just… talk to her before you slap the cuffs on her, okay?"

They took two wrong turns before Wy spotted a street sign leaning up against a telephone pole. The white letters on the green sign were faded but legible. "Mainsail Avenue," Wy said, pointing.

Liam turned left and immediately the road went from a two-lane paved blacktop to a one-lane, continuous buffalo wallow. Liam wasn't prepared for the first dip and bounced both of them off the roof of the cab. "I'm guessing not a borough-maintained road," Wy said, grabbing the handle and hanging on for dear life. "This is worse than that goat track that leads to the judge's house."

He slowed down to a crawl, which helped a little. The trees overgrew the road to where their branches whapped the pickup's rear views hard enough to move them so far out of alignment that he couldn't see behind him. Not that he could have anyway. It was as if the sun had set three hours early.

Mainsail Avenue was fairly straight for about half a mile, when it ended in a cross street called Reefpoint, so marked by another faded sign, and saw their first house, followed by six more equally spaced along the road that stretched an equal distance either side of Mainsail. "One-acre lots, you think?"

"Looks like," Wy said.

"And fighting the vegetation back every minute of every day. Noon is probably the only time these people see daylight."

Reefpoint climbed to Halyard, where another six houses were carefully spaced out along its length. Halyard climbed higher, with a switchback thrown in, and ended at Turnbuckle. "What were the roads that Sybilla said led to Crow's Nest?"

"Telltale, then Backstay," Wy said. "She called it an aerie. I think we're good if we just keep going up."

Sure enough, Turnbuckle ended in Telltale, this time after two switchbacks and a decrepit wooden bridge over a narrow creek.

"Did your ears just pop?" Wy said.

"Uh-huh." Liam wrestled the truck around another hairpin turn and up another switchback. He checked the indicators for engine temperature. Nothing in the red so far. "If they lost some of these trees..."

"I was thinking the same."

Here the houses were smaller and closer together and built only on the right, or up side of the street. "Developer must have run out of money," Liam said.

Backstay had no homes at all on it that they could see,

but the amount of fill necessary to put in a foundation would have beggared anyone who wasn't a billionaire. The ground now fell so steeply away from the road that they caught glimpses of the view they had both imagined and it promised exceedingly fair.

There was no street sign at Crow's Nest but it was the only turn remaining so they took it, another hard hairpin right. The grade was so steep Liam shifted into low and let up on the gas very slowly. "I don't think they have to worry about being burglarized." He wondered how big a turnaround there was at the top. He was definitely turning in his miles for this case.

They rocked and rolled for another interminable five minutes. It was a relief when they finally topped out on a narrow flat of gravel carved from the wall of the bluff. The top of the bluff and Heavenly Drive were less than a hundred feet above.

A tiny log cabin was built flush against the face of the bluff. To the right there was an outhouse and to the left a six-by-six garden plot where the cabbages and Brussels sprouts were doing well.

Liam had stopped and Wy reached for the door handle. "Wait," Liam said. He backed and filled until he had the truck pointing downhill again. "Okay, you get out and stay here. Crow's Nest went a little way the other direction at Backstay. I'm going to leave the truck there and walk back up."

Wy nodded. If Ms. Petroff saw the truck in front of the cabin she might run for it. She got out and Liam inched over the edge of the rise and out of sight. He'd left the truck in low and she could hear it grinding its way down the hill. Better his truck than her Subaru.

Before her Chungasqak Bay stretched from left to right with the Kenai Mountains lining the southern horizon in full relief. It was very nearly the same view out their new front window, just a little lower, and she wondered if custom would ever stale its infinite variety. She couldn't imagine it. She knew in her head that the mountains were four and five thousand feet higher than where she stood, but her eyes told her she was level with their summits. Every white-topped crag and crest was clearly outlined against a sky going a rich, deep blue. The lagoon, inlets, bays, and fjords that lined the coast below cast dark, mysterious shadows on their waters. Lights twinkled from only a few far-flung locations. There were more lights scattered about the Bay, boats on the way home after a day's fishing.

She turned to look at the cabin. It had been made from logs a long time ago, and those logs had not been oiled in a long time. The roof was covered with a thick mat of vegetation that was more than moss and might even flower in the summer. The front door was offset to the right, and on the left was a large picture window. Wy couldn't imagine how they'd gotten the glass up here without breaking it.

She walked to the door and knocked. "Hello? Hello, is anyone home?"

There was no answer. She reached for the handle and the door opened easily inwards. Inside was a single room, about sixteen feet by twenty, where a full-size bed took up most of one corner. A wood stove sat in the opposite corner with two easy chairs flanking it. A small dining table with two chairs sat in front of the window and a kitchen area consisting of a high, freestanding counter with shelves beneath stood against the wall in back of the door. There were two more windows, sliders with screens, one on each side.

A propane lantern hung from a hook and she took it down and pumped it up and lit it with matches she found in an ashtray on the table. With the gloom dispelled more details revealed themselves. The cabin might be old but it was clean and neat, with none of the funky smell that came with age in so many of its brethren. There were two sets of shelves, Blazo boxes three high each, one for clothes and one for books. There was a five-gallon water jug on the floor under the counter and a small metal tub on top with toiletries neatly arranged around it. A rectangular mirror in a plastic frame hung on the wall. The shelves below held a selection of canned and dry goods, heavy on the Spam, and a flat of bottled water. There was a saucepan, a frying pan, a moka pot, and a two-burner Coleman stove. On a single shelf nailed to the wall above sat two plates, three bowls, and a collection of public radio mugs. A rusting coffee can held cutlery and utensils. A small wooden box with a lid that locked held a bag of ground coffee and packets of raw sugar and creamer.

There was a nightstand next to the bed. On it was a headlamp and a stack of books, including a fat textbook on fossils in east Africa by Maeve Leakey, a tattered paperback copy of *The Lincoln Lawyer* by Michael Connelly, the first three novels of the Codex Alera series by Jim Butcher, Willie Hensley's autobiography, and a slim volume titled *Mapping the Americas* by Shari M. Huhndorf, subtitled "The Transnational Politics of Contemporary Native Culture." It was published by Cornell University Press and looked dense but interesting.

She put the book down and looked around the cabin again. She thought she would have liked Erik Berglund, too, and she was suddenly angry that the pleasure of his acquaintance had been stolen from her, and that the community of Alaska had been robbed of the contributions that he might have made to it, and that the world of archeology would now never benefit from his discoveries. Murder was the rankest form of crime, the outright theft of a human life and all that that life had to offer to family, friends, and the world.

There was a step and she turned to see Liam in the doorway, red-faced, sweating, and breathing hard. "They do not pay me enough to ever again walk up that hill."

"Did you manage to hide the Penis Extender?"

He nodded. "Backstay does go farther west, but you can't see it because the trees have almost overgrown it. I backed in. You can't even see it's there." He looked down, saw the flat of bottled water, and grabbed one. Twisting off the cap he tilted his head back and flatfooted it. Still breathing hard he put the cap back on and looked around for the garbage. It was in a small pail with a tight lid.

"You liked this guy," she said.

He considered while he got his breathing under control. "Yes," he said. "Yes, I did. He was a good guy, smart, funny, interesting, really into his job. He had that ability to reduce words of six syllables into words of two syllables so that non-experts could understand what the hell he was saying. I don't know if he'd found what he said he had but he was excited about it and was sure he could prove it. I've always like people with a cause." He looked around the cabin. "Did you find anything?"

"He was a reader. And he wasn't a slob, in spite of living rough. I've seen a lot worse."

He went to the table and looked through the scant stack of paper there. "He only had one Visa card in his wallet, along with his driver's license and an ATM card." He let the paperwork fall with a sigh. "Ads. He must have picked them up at the store. Did you see a checkbook?"

She shook her head. "He could have paid for everything through his bank online and elected not to receive paper statements. There are probably computers and Wi-Fi at the library."

"What's this?" He pulled something from the back of one of the chairs.

"What's what?" She came to stand next to him.

It was a bright scarf made of lightweight cotton, at one end a vivid pink which by the other end had graduated to a pale peach. "Pretty," he said. "And for sure it didn't belong to Erik."

They both heard it at the same time. "What does Ms. Petroff drive?"

"An old Ford Jeep." He listened. "Sounds like it's in pretty good shape. Turn down the lamp." He replaced the scarf on the back of the chair. She hung the lamp back up on the hook. "Let's wait around the back of the cabin."

They did so, listening to the engine of the car grind ever closer, until it topped the rise and the driver killed the engine, which rattled and popped and shook and dieseled for a good minute afterward. Wy, pressed against Liam, heard his heart beating in one ear and the sound of a car door opening and closing in the other. Light footsteps, then the creaking of the cabin door as it opened. Liam pulled away from her and went around the cabin on soundless feet. Wy followed as quietly as she could.

He went in the cabin first and surprised Ms. Petroff in the act of lighting the gas lantern. "Oh!" she said, and knocked the lantern off the table. Liam caught it before it hit the floor. Ms. Petroff made an abortive attempt to reach the door, and only subsided when she saw Wy standing there.

"Sit down, Ms. Petroff," Liam said, taking her firmly by one arm and guiding her to a chair at the table. Wy came in and closed the door behind her, and Liam finished lighting the lamp. He turned it up all the way, filling the little room with a warm radiance. He hung it from the hook and they both turned to look at the girl.

She was sitting with her elbows on the table and her face in her hands. The scarf was looped around her neck. "You lied to me, Ms. Petroff," Liam said, his voice implacable. "I asked you where Erik Berglund's cabin was and you said you didn't know."

She took a deep, shuddering breath, and dropped her hands, revealing a tear-stained face. She sat back and folded her hands in her lap. "Yes, sir, I did."

"Why?"

She swallowed. "I didn't want you to know I knew."

"Because I'd have questions you don't want to answer."

She closed her eyes. "Yes, sir."

"Did you have a relationship with Erik Berglund, Ms. Petroff?"

She bit her lip and another tear slid down her cheek. "Yes."

"Where were you between Monday night at ten and two a.m. Tuesday morning?"

Her eyes flew open. "What?"

"Where were you between—"

"Stop!" she shouted. It was the first loss of self-possession Liam had observed in her. "Just stop. I didn't kill Erik. I was nowhere near his dig that night or even that day. My aunt and uncle had a family picnic on the beach and we were out there until after sunset." She let out a long, shuddering sigh. "Yes, I had a relationship with Erik, but it's not what you think."

"What was it, then?"

"He—" She twisted her hands together. "He was my father."

They stared at her, speechless.

She'd taken an online genealogy course because she'd thought it would be fun if she constructed a family tree for her parents' anniversary. When the instructor suggested all the students take a DNA test from 23andMe, she didn't hesitate. When the results came back, she didn't believe them, and submitted a second sample, which came back the same.

Alexei Petroff wasn't her father.

What felt even weirder was that she was half white. She had been raised as a full-blooded Sugpiaq. It was how she was down in the tribal register.

She had confronted her mother, who had confirmed this unwelcome news but wouldn't tell Sally who her birth father was. Alexei, her mother said, didn't know.

Liam thought of the barely repressed rage he'd observed in Alexei and wondered if that was true. Sally Petroff unconsciously confirmed that feeling when she said, "I don't know if she's right about that. Dad always treated me a little differently than my brothers. I thought it was because I was a girl and they were boys. Dad's a really traditional guy and he's all about the men doing the providing and the women catering to them. He was mad at me when I decided to go away to school."

Pissed at losing all that unpaid domestic help, Wy thought, and was immediately ashamed of herself. A traditional lifestyle was why Alaska Natives had survived millennia in some of the most difficult natural conditions on earth, and there was no call to disrespect the people who still lived by those precepts. Their traditions were responsible for the existence of the Yupiq part of her DNA. She had been raised by white adoptive parents and she had never lived a traditional lifestyle, and while she might have written off her relatives in Ik'iki'ka she knew what she owed the people who came before them.

Besides, Alexei might have been angry but he hadn't forbidden his daughter to leave the village. He could have, and he could have made it stick, too.

"There's an online database that collates DNA samples. Even if the DNA of the person you're looking for isn't in it, sometimes you can trace them through the DNA of a relative of theirs whose is."

Erik had a second cousin in the database, and the connection was made.

"It took me a long time to find him. He was in eastern Africa, working for UNESCO. I wrote to him. The next thing I knew he was here, in Blewestown."

"This was in June?"

She nodded. "He wrote to me that he was here. I told my mother. She was really angry, and she told me if I told Dad that she would never forgive me." She wiped her face dry with her hands and met Liam's eyes. "Erik told me Mom never told him about me. He never even knew I existed, that he had a child. He told me he came back to the Bay to meet me, for us to get to know each other. I didn't transfer down here until a month ago, like I told you, but he would drive to Anchorage once a week and we would meet for a meal or a walk. When I moved back to the Bay, we would meet here and talk. That's all. That's really all."

"That scarf."

She touched it. "Erik brought it back from Africa for me." Her lip trembled. It would be the only thing she ever received from the hands of her birth father. "I forgot it the last time I was here."

"Do you think your mother told Alexei that Erik was your father?"

"She would never."

"Do you think Erik told Alexei he was your father?"

"No!" This time she was shouting. "No, he didn't. He promised, and I believed him. Nobody told Dad anything, not Mom, not Erik, not me." She sniffled, and Wy looked around for Kleenex and settled for a paper towel. Sally mopped her eyes and blew her nose and crumpled the towel between her hands. "We talked about it. Erik didn't want to meet in secret." Her lips trembled into a smile. "He was proud of me. Proud that he had a daughter. I think I—" Her voice broke. "I think I could have loved him. If we'd had time, maybe we could have made Dad understand."

And now all she had left was a scarf and a dead hero to worship. No substitute for a living, breathing father, even if Sally's mother had treated him as nothing more than a sperm donor. "When was the last time you saw Erik?"

"Sunday. I came up in the morning with doughnuts and

coffee. He wanted me to come down to the dig. He said he'd used the dig as an excuse, something he could pretend to work at so he could stay here and see me. He said that he'd found something unexpected, something that would refute prior studies and add to the history of the Sugpiaq in the Bay."

"Did he tell you anything about his personal finances?" Liam held up a hand. "I'm not accusing you of anything, Ms. Petroff. I'm just trying to find a paper trail to inform my investigation, so I can find out who killed him." He gestured at the table. "So far as I can tell he didn't even have a checkbook."

She sat down again and took a deep breath. "He didn't have many possessions. He said when you spent time in places like east Africa, you understood how much we have that we don't need. Clothes and food and shelter were necessities." She glanced at the bookshelf and smiled a little. "He said books were a luxury he couldn't do without. He said once he spent more money on books than everything else combined."

"How did he pay for them?"

"When he was working for UNESCO, he said they paid him by wire deposit into his bank. He charged everything to his Visa card or paid with cash out of an ATM, and paid his bills with automated payment processing through his checking account." She smiled faintly. "No stamps, he said." Her hand caressed the scarf again, gently, reverently. "I barely got to know him. Just a few months, and now he's gone." Her voice broke.

"What do you know about your father's brother, Joshua?" Liam said.

She looked up, blinking away tears. "What?"

"Your uncle Joshua, your father's brother. What do you know about him?"

"I—I—I guess I know what everyone knows. He disappeared when he was ten years old."

"Did you know that Erik was with him when he disappeared?"

"Yes, and I know Erik was attacked at the same time and due to a traumatic brain injury that he was never able to remember what happened that day. Erik told me."

"You asked him about it?"

"Of course. It was one of the first things we talked about."

"And you believed him."

She drew herself up and Liam saw a resurgence of the Ms. Petroff of old, and, truthfully, was glad of it. "Of course."

Liam looked at Wy. Wy shrugged. "Okay, Ms. Petroff. I'll be talking to your aunt and uncle to confirm your presence at the picnic, but that's all for now."

She raised her chin and met his eyes squarely. "Am I fired, sir?"

"Did you go through my desk, Ms. Petroff?"

Her shoulders slumped a little, and then straightened again. "I did, sir. I wanted to see what your thoughts were on Erik's murder."

He stared out the window for a long time with no appreciation for the view. Finally he looked back at her. "I'm a cop, Ms. Petroff. People lie to me all day long every day on the job. I expect the truth from the people I work with. I rely on it. I can't do my job without it." He stared at her.

There was a chin wobble, instantly repressed. "I understand, sir. I'll clean out my desk in the morning."

"You'll show up for work at eight a.m. and do your job," he said firmly, "and every day afterward."

"Sir?"

"You heard me, Ms. Petroff." He met her eyes with a hard stare. "Don't let me down again."

She stood up and held out her hand. "I won't, sir."

They shook on it. Ms. Petroff got in her Jeep and crept down the hill while Wy and Liam extinguished the lantern and made sure the door was on the latch. Liam had been right; there was no lock.

They stepped out into the soft fall evening and stood in the middle of the small, cleared area. "Gloriosky," Wy said.

Liam, like her, surveying the view, couldn't disagree. The sun was an hour away from setting but it was setting at their backs, so that the light was crawling up the Kenai Mountains and leaching away into the deepening blue of the sky. Termination dust encroached only on the very peaks so far. The light of a boat approached the head of the Spit, making for the boat harbor and home. If there was a swell on the water's surface it was hidden by distance.

"The first time I met Sybilla I took her back to the post," Liam said.

"Yes?"

"She asked Ms. Petroff how her father was. Ms. Petroff said he was fine, and Sybilla said, 'Such a nice boy, Erik. So polite.'" He looked at Wy. "Sybilla knew Erik was Sally Petroff's father."

"She was a teacher. They always know everything. She said she warned him. I'll bet it had something to do with not stirring up old trouble."

"Yeah, and see how well that turned out," he said. "I knew she reminded me of someone the first time I saw her. Erik had given me a tour of his dig the day before, and I didn't put it together. Some detective, me."

"You got me off the hook, not once but twice. Your detecting skills are okay by me."

He put his arm around Wy and pulled her in, smiling into her upturned face. "I love you."

She smiled back. "I love you, too. And the sooner we're home the sooner I can demonstrate how much."

"Motivation," he said. "I fear for the springs on my Penis Extender."

There was a rustle from the side of the clearing and they looked around to see a lynx with five kittens coalesce out of the undergrowth. They took no notice of Liam and Wy, and the two of them stood very still, watching the dappled cats with their enormous paws pad silently by, to melt into a copse of scrub spruce as if by magic.

Wy let out her breath in a long sigh. "That was worth moving here all by itself."

"I know," Liam said. "Basically all the wildlife I remember from Newenham is the fish."

"And the raven."

"Bite your tongue."

Hand in hand they started walking toward the steep slide of pitted gravel that passed for a road.

There was a soft squawk from the top of a tree and Liam stopped so fast his heel skidded in the dirt. "What was that?"

They looked around but whatever it was made no further noise, and they were left to continue on their way in peace.

Twenty

Monday, September 9

MONDAY MORNING LIAM WALKED INTO the post to find Ms. Petroff at her desk. "Good morning, sir."

"Good morning. All well here?"

"It's only one minute after eight, sir."

"Ms. Petroff, did you just make a joke?"

"I might have, sir, but I take no responsibility for how well your ears work."

"Less of your sass, Ms. Petroff."

"Yes, sir."

He hung his ball cap on the coatrack and sat behind his desk. The folder holding the square and his scribbled notes on each person of interest were exactly where he'd left them in the drawer on Friday. He pulled it out and spread everything across his desk once more.

On Saturday morning he had spoken with Ms. Petroff's

aunt and uncle, and they had confirmed that she was indeed at the picnic on the beach on Monday evening and gone home with them when it ended. Evidently everyone in Blewestown who wasn't at Gabe McGuire's party had spent the afternoon and evening on the beach in a last gasp of summer celebration—maybe the beach party was a reward for the morning march—and there were hundreds more witnesses who could attest as to her whereabouts. He added her name to the outer edge of the square, on the other side of her parents.

On Sunday afternoon Wy had flown him back to Kapilat for a second interview with Alexei and Kimberley Petroff. Kimberley had answered the door and very nearly slammed it in his face.

"Let him in, Kimberley," Alexei said from behind her. He sounded tired.

They settled into the living room again in what was apparently now their assigned seating, although this time Kimberley sat down on the couch next to Alexei. Liam leaned forward with his elbows on his knees, running the band of his ball cap through his fingers. "Mr. Petroff, I understand you lost a brother thirty years ago."

Alexei's eyes widened. "Yes."

"He was ten years old?"

Alexei felt for Kimberley's hand, his eyes never leaving Liam's face. "Yes."

"I've read the file and the article in the local newspaper, but could you run that day down for me, please?"

Alexei swallowed. "He and Erik were across the Bay with both our parents on a shopping trip. They told the boys they could take the skiff for a run, and they ended up on Sand Beach. Erik was attacked and left unconscious, and Josh disappeared." He swallowed. "He was never found."

Liam took a deep breath and let it out slowly. "The skeleton of a ten-year-old boy has been found near where Erik Berglund's body was found." Kimberley made a sound and Alexei pulled her in tight.

Liam pulled a small, heavyweight manila envelope from his pocket. He unwound the string that secured the flap and produced a glass tube with a swab inside. "You are, I believe, his nearest living relative?"

"Yes," Alexei said, staring at the tube. "Both our parents are dead."

There had already been one unwelcome surprise revealed to this family from DNA this year, and Liam was sorry to have to foist a second on them, but it was the only way. He held up the tube. "If we could have a sample of your DNA, the medical examiner could test it against that of the skeleton's. Then we would know."

Alexei appeared hypnotized by the sight of the tube. "How long will it take?"

"One to three days, depending on how backed up things are at the lab."

"And then we'll know."

Liam nodded. "Yes."

Alexei looked from the tube to Liam. "How did he die?"

Liam could feel himself stiffening, and made an effort to relax. "I'm sorry to say he did not die of natural causes."

"He was murdered."

It wasn't a question, but Liam answered it anyway. "Yes."

"How?"

Liam could have made the standard answer, that the case was under investigation and the details were confidential until that investigation was concluded, but he could not bring himself to do so to this man who had lost his only brother thirty years before. "Blunt force trauma. A blow to the head."

"It would have been quick, then."

Liam sure as hell hoped so. "I believe so."

"Who kills a kid?" Alexei said, his face contorting. "Who the hell kills a ten-year-old kid out beachcombing on a sunny summer day? And leaves another one for dead?" He bent his head for a moment, blinking. Kimberley put her arm around his shoulders and tucked her head beneath his chin.

When he looked up again he was dry-eyed and determined. He jerked his chin at the tube. "What do I do?"

⚶

Now, on Monday morning, Liam looked down at the square, dissatisfied all over again. The square thing always worked. He willed it to do so again.

Alexei and Kimberley Petroff were cleared, as Sergei Pete had confirmed.

Domenica Garland's Zoom meeting had checked out, too. It was the first time Liam had direct-dialed Europe. Her boss had sounded as if he were in the next room.

Gabe McGuire had Len Needham for an alibi, although that was dicey since Len was also a close relative. But McGuire had zero motive. Liam had contacted the relevant authority at the borough and Gabe's petition to vacate the right of way was on track to being approved and had been before Erik Berglund was murdered.

Hilary Houten might have had motive but he came and left with Blue Jay Jefferson and let's face it, the guy was in his eighties and he couldn't get around without a honking big cane to hold him up. He wasn't going to pick a physical fight with anyone.

Same went for Blue Jay.

Liam sat back and tossed down the pencil. He scrubbed his hands through his hair and swiveled to look out the window behind his desk. The view was somewhat obscured by the inevitable alders and ragged black spruce but there was enough room that he could see a slice of the Bay and the mountains beyond.

He wondered if he'd made a mistake in accepting the Blewestown post. In Newenham he would have been out on a call already and catching up on three more from the day before. Of course he had been for a long time almost the only law enforcement officer within three hundred or more miles, so there was that. And he had been getting tired of the sameness of the job, the constant domestic violence calls, the drunk and disorderlies, the reported break-ins by tweakers looking for anything to sell so they could buy their next fix. Everybody remembered the murders because murder was high profile, the stuff of crime fiction and Hollywood blockbusters, but it was the daily grind of seeing his fellow citizens at their worst that wore him down. That wore them all down.

One of the first things Wy had asked him when they met— it was one of the first things everyone asked—was why he had become a trooper. "For the uniform," he had said, which was what he always said. It was flippant and flirty and non-responsive. It was also in some small part true. He'd grown up idolizing the Alaska State Troopers because they just looked so damn cool in their Smokey hats. He looked at his button-down flannel and jeans. His first official day on the job in Blewestown and he wasn't wearing one. There were three clean, pressed, perfectly tailored uniforms hanging in the closet at home. What did that say?

He wondered just how quick Barton was imagining he could slide Liam into a job at HQ in Anchorage. Back in the day it had been the height of Liam's ambition to ascend the ladder to Barton's job, boss of the whole damn shooting match. There had been a time when he'd kept a secret list of all the improvements he would make to the agency if he were in charge. Jenny, his first wife, had been enthusiastically in support of his ambitions and aided and abetted them with formal dinners featuring movers and shakers, luncheons with their spouses, and letters of support to legislators who ran on law-and-order platforms. She'd named Charlie after Liam's father and made sure to mention Charlie's grandfather and namesake, Air Force Colonel Charles Bradley Campbell, to every soldier and airman she met who was stationed at JBER. She had been the perfect partner for that Liam.

This Liam, not so much. He wondered if Jim was right and he should pull the plug, or at least start planning for it. State troopers were well paid and the time he had served in the Bush would amp up his pension admirably, and he was pretty sure Wy still had the first dime she'd ever made. They wouldn't be rich but they would be comfortable. He could learn how to hunt and fish, fill the freezer every year. Maybe travel some. He hadn't been out of the country since college.

God, that sounded boring. He wondered what Wy was doing, and what she was wearing, and how quickly he could get her out of it that evening.

They had woken up that morning to make love, do form on their new deck, showered together, made pancakes and eaten them together, and he'd left her reluctantly when it was time to go to work. But then that was always the case. She had disappeared out of his life once. He didn't ever want that to happen again, and some part of him lived in fear that she would.

The window was open and a mild, cool breeze carried in the scents of autumn, woodsmoke, unpicked berries rotting on the vine, fallen leaves decomposing. He heard a noise like the sound of someone knocking on a metal door. He looked around to meet the beady black eyes of a huge raven sitting on a spruce bough almost exactly level with his gaze.

"Fuck," he said.

"Kraaaack—kraaaaaaaack," the raven said.

The bird wore coal-colored feathers that looked as if they'd been oiled. He was at minimum two and a half feet beak to tail and had fed well enough this past summer that he significantly bent the branch he was sitting on.

"I thought I left you behind," Liam said. "Like a long fucking way behind. Like far enough behind I wouldn't have to put up with you anymore."

"Koo-kluck-kluck-kloo-kluck," quoth the raven.

"Do it to me again and again" Donna Summer sang behind him.

"Kraaack!" With one beat of his iridescent wings the raven was aloft and gone.

Liam spun around and picked up his phone. "Hey, Brillo."

"Yeah, yeah, happy fucking Monday to you, too, Campbell."

At least he wasn't operating at a Barton decibel level today. "You have the results back from the DNA?"

"Yeah, the kid is definitely Joshua Petroff."

"How soon can you release the body? His family wants him home."

"As soon as I sign off on the paperwork."

"Let me know and I'll send Wy to pick him up."

"Yeah, listen, I got something else going on here. Something weird."

"Weird?"

"Yeah, weird. As in freaky, creepy, spooky. Weird. I told you how the kid died, somebody bashed his head in."

"I remember."

"Yeah, well, I think the same weapon that killed the kid was used to kill Erik Berglund."

Liam sat up so fast he pushed himself away from the desk and banged off the windowsill behind him. "What?"

"I told you, weird, right? There's a kind of corner, almost but not quite a right angle to the impact depression in both of the skulls. I measured and it's almost exactly the same size in both. It's higher up on the kid and lower down on Berglund, but I'm pretty sure the same thing was used both times."

"You realize Joshua Petroff and Erik Berglund were killed thirty years apart?"

Brillo sounded testy. "I can read a report."

"Are you sure the wound on Berglund's head wasn't from the old injury?"

"What the hell, Campbell? I told you the old injury had healed to the point I could barely tell where it was, let alone what caused it. Oh, and if you could get your other girlfriend the hell out of my hair, I'd be grateful."

"My other—"

"The scribbler. She's been on me about this PM the whole goddamn week. She annoys me even more than you do and that's saying something." Brillo hung up.

Liam let the phone drop into its cradle and picked his jaw up off the floor. He looked down at the square.

Couldn't get around without a cane.

But Blue Jay Jefferson had been with him that night.

As if Liam's thought had conjured him out of the ether, the door to his office opened and Blue Jay Jefferson thumped in with his walker. He didn't look happy. He was carrying Hilary Houten's cane and he dropped it on Liam's desk. It knocked the phone out of its cradle and then the entire phone crashed to the floor.

Over his shoulder Ms. Petroff said, "I'm sorry, sir, I tried to stop him."

"It's all right, Ms. Petroff. As you were."

She disappeared without closing the door.

Liam picked up the phone and set it back on the desk. There was a chip out of the handset but there was still a dial tone. He put it back in its cradle and looked up. "You have something you want to tell me, Mr. Jefferson?"

"I didn't know about the kids," Jefferson said, and sat down.

꙳

"Hil came back across the Bay with me after the Chamber do," Jefferson said. His face was set, his mouth a straight line.

"That afternoon Garvey Halloran came over on his Bayliner. He's a volunteer for the fire department, and he was there when you pulled that skeleton out of the cave." Some emotion must have crossed Liam's face because Jefferson snorted. "Garvey went to school with my kids. They're all living Outside now so Garvey checks in on me. Since he's a first responder, I get all the news first and firsthand. Ain't no secrets in a small town."

There were no secrets in Alaska period, Liam thought. "Mr. Jefferson—"

"It's Tom," Jefferson said. "That Blue Jay crap got hung on me by the newspapers, and it sure as hell ain't Mr. Jefferson. Let me finish, Sergeant, and then I'll answer any questions you got." Jefferson thought about the ramifications of that all-encompassing statement for a moment and added, "Mostly."

"All right."

"So, Garvey told us about finding the skeleton." Jeff shook his head and sighed. "I never see a man go so white. I don't think Garvey noticed. Leastways he didn't say anything. After Garvey left I tackled Hil about it. He wouldn't say nothing at first. For days he was practically mute. I don't think he was sleeping, like at all. Then last night I poured myself my usual sun over the yardarm tot and Hil asked me to pour him one, too." Jefferson fixed Liam with a piercing yellow eye, his resemblance to a bald eagle even more pronounced. "Understand, Sergeant, I've known Hil for forty years and I never see him take a drink. He never said why, he just never did. I always figured him for an alkie, or maybe just a teetotaler." He shrugged. "Didn't matter to me. But last night he asks for a drink. So I pour him one and we sit down in front of the fireplace to plan out how to fix the world like we always do. He takes a gulp and his hand is shaking like a seven-point-four and he coughs and chokes and wheezes, and then by god, he takes another.

"And then, Sergeant, he starts to talk." Jefferson settled back in the chair, his face grim. "Only thing you gotta understand about Hil, Sergeant, is that paper he wrote forty years ago on human settlement in the Bay made him. He got wrote up everywhere, he was on television when most of the people watching couldn't have understood one word in ten he said, he won some shovelbum award. They give him that."

He pointed at the cane. Liam followed his eyes and for the first time saw the tiny rectangle of brass screwed to the handle's brace. It was inscribed with Houten's name and a date and the words "For Distinguished Archeological Achievement."

"It never left his hand after that, whether his arthritis was giving him a bad time or not," Jefferson said. "His reputation was made and all the resource companies wanted him on retainer for his bona fide expert opinion on how none of the places they wanted to dig or drill would have any impact on the Alaska Native culture or ever had any importance in Alaska Native history. He never had to do another lick of real work, just opine. Hil was fucking great with opinions that sounded authoritative enough to shut down every greenie and tree hugger who raised a voice in opposition." He shook his head. "He was something back in the day, before he got old. Before we all got old."

"So when Erik Berglund came along this year, promising to refute all of Houten's findings…"

Jefferson gave a curt not. "I figured it was professional jealousy, and hell, look at the two of them. One was on his way out, old, obstinate, opinionated, had no truck with or respect for the Sugpiaq. The other grew up on the other side of the Bay smack damn in the middle of them, young, smart, familiar with all the new scientific techniques or what the fuck ever, had a relationship with UNESCO and was threatening to pitch them on making the Bay a World Heritage Site or some goddamn such." He rolled his eyes. "I don't think there's a hope in hell of that ever happening and I don't think Erik did, either, but it's what they was arguing about at Gabe's party. Man was nice enough to give us a front row seat to the next blockbuster months before anyone else was going to get to see it and these two yahoos are ruining the party. I think Erik just wanted to poke the bear. They shut up when I went over to shut them up."

"And after the party?"

Jefferson's jaw tightened. "Hil wanted to wait for Erik to come out so he could finish the argument. Nothing I could say to talk him out of it. By the time Erik come out everyone else had gone. Hil got out of my pickup and started yelling. Erik laughed at him and turned his back and walked in the direction of the trail head. Hil went after him, thumping along with his cane. It was dark enough by then that I give it only a couple of minutes before I went after him. I found him standing alone at the trail head, leaning on that cane and vibrating like a shaker table on a gold dredge. Erik was nowhere to be seen. Hil said he'd gone down the trail, was going to sleep at the dig. So we went back to the harbor and bunked on my boat, and went home the next morning."

He looked at Liam, defiance in every line of his face. "You'll notice I never told you about that when you asked what went on at the party."

"I noticed."

"Never would have, either."

"No."

Something about Liam's certainty that Blue Jay Jefferson did not snitch on his friends seemed to put heart into the old fart. "And then last night," he said, and stopped.

"Houten started talking," Liam said when it appeared Jefferson needed a prompt.

Jefferson took in a deep breath and let it out slowly. "Yeah. All about his fucking monograph and how Erik had been trying to ruin his reputation since he was a fat little brat."

Liam started putting the pieces together in his mind and almost knew what Jefferson was going to say next.

"Hil found the cave thirty years ago. Just like Erik he figured out that the old folks used that spur of rock for a dock. He found the cave—he got around better back then—and he found the artifacts inside it.

"The problem was he didn't know anything about them at the time he wrote his paper ten years before, after which it was way too late for a man like Hil to climb down. He knew he had to get rid of the artifacts, because if someone found them everything he'd ever done would be called into question. He was about to load up when he heard the kids' voices from the beach. The Petroff boy was first in the cave and Hil panicked and hit him. He went out after Erik. Erik ran but he held on to his baby fat until puberty burned it off and at ten years he couldn't run very fast, so Hil caught up with him, gimp and all, and laid him out, too." He nodded at the cane. "That thing is not just another pretty face."

Liam didn't smile.

Jefferson shook his head. "Hil said he thought he'd killed him, Erik. He was terrified when he heard the boy was still alive, and so relieved when he heard he couldn't remember anything about that day. I think he was always afraid he might, though. I think it was always in his mind."

"What did he do afterward?"

If possible, Jefferson looked even grimmer. "This ain't easy to tell and won't be easy to hear. Hil went back into the cave and he, well, he made the boy's body fit through that crack in the wall. Garvey told me about it and I don't know how Hil managed, but he did."

"Why didn't he at least drag Erik's body into the cave?"

"Got spooked, said he heard voices." Jefferson shrugged. "Probably his imagination. He was scared enough telling the story, I expect he was fucking terrified at the time. He wasn't ever a man prone to violence, Sergeant, especially since he never in his life had enough muscle to punch a hole through so much as a Kleenex. I reckon the situation just got away from him."

Pudgy little brat. There had been more than disgust at Erik's pudginess, Liam thought. The reason Hilary Houten had left Erik where he had fallen was that Houten knew he couldn't fit him through the crack. Liam willed his imagination away from that image only to be immediately assaulted by another.

The *Shawshank* hammer. Houten would have used it to break up the boy's body enough to feed it through the crack. "And then?" was all he said.

Jefferson, eying him with caution, said, "And then he left. He didn't even take the things he found in the cave with him, which mighta saved Erik's life that time around. And he never told anyone. Until last night."

A brief silence. "Where is Mr. Houten now?"

The old fart stared at him. "Didn't I say? He's dead. He only had the one drink but it made him sick as a dog afterward. I had to hold his head over the toilet and muscle him into bed. He passed right out." He shook his head. "He always gets up when he smells the coffee. This morning he didn't. I went in and he was dead. Already cold. His heart just gave out, I figure. Confession ain't always good for the soul, you know." He shifted in his chair. "I brung his body back in the boat, and called Fiona. He's with her now, waiting on your call."

He nodded at the cane. "I expect those voodoo techs you law enforcement types got nowadays can find traces of Berglund's blood on the handle."

Liam had recorded Jefferson's entire statement on his

phone. He gave it to Ms. Petroff to transcribe. Jefferson balanced a pair of cheaters with purple plastic frames on the very end of his nose, read it through carefully beginning to end, and signed.

He pulled himself to his feet with his walker and resettled the Blewestown Ballers ball cap more firmly on his head, causing the white tufts of hair at the sides to stand straight out perpendicular to the cap's edge. Unlike Sybilla Karlsen, he'd aged beyond vanity. He stared out Liam's window and spoke in a reminiscent voice. "You should have seen this place back in the day. Bay was filled with shrimp and salmon and king crab, canneries on both shores, fishing boats all over the damn place. Bars busting out all up and down the streets and young men flush with cash blowing it all on girls and booze. Japanese buyers lining up all the way to Soldotna to buy anything we could pull out of the water." He looked in the direction of RPetCo's rig. "And now it's gonna be oil wells and rigs up and down the Bay, and probably spills, and no self-respecting fish is ever gonna want to spawn in a stream in these parts ever again."

He turned and looked at Liam. "What happens now?"

Blue Jay Jefferson was a man who took his medicine straight, no chaser. "At best you're guilty of obstruction of justice. At worst, you're an accessory after the fact."

The old man drew himself up as straight as his aged spine would allow and glared at Liam. "Good luck proving that, Sergeant. I didn't see a goddamn thing and you can't prove I did. I'm the only witness left alive."

Liam looked at him for a long moment. "I'll run it by the judge," he said, and then he said, "Oh hell. Go home, old man. I know where you live."

Jefferson had one foot over the threshold when Liam said, "Tom."

The old man looked over his shoulder.

"Why did you tell me? You didn't have to."

Blue Jay Jefferson tugged fiercely at the bill of his cap, pulling it even tighter to his head and causing his remaining hairs to make him look even more like the Scarecrow after the Wizard stuffed his head with brains. "I told you," he said. "I didn't know about the kids."

*

"How do you feel about all this?" Wy said that evening. They were curled up on the couch, watching the mountains turn an even darker blue and the Bay itself fade to black.

"Kind of pissed off, you want to know the truth," Liam said. "Two murders, one attempt, and the perp dies on me before I get to charge him."

"Anticlimactic," she said.

"Kinda."

"But nobody shot at you," she said.

"And I didn't have to jump out of any airplanes."

"Or jump out of any boats."

"Or fall down any glaciers. I never even took my sidearm out of the glove compartment. Am I still in Alaska or what?"

"And you didn't mess up another uniform."

"There is that."

She raised her head to look at him. "Are you ever going to put one on again?"

Twenty-One

Sunday, September 15

THEY WERE SUMMONED TO TEA WITH Sybilla the following Sunday in her room at Sunset Heights. Having been given a heads up by Liz, Wy was wearing the only dress she owned, a sunny yellow sleeveless cotton sheath with a scoop neck. She'd bought it to wear at her college graduation, mostly to make her parents happy, and worn it a second time at her wedding. It was a little wrinkled because upon seeing her in it Liam had immediately tried to get her out of it again.

Liam, because what the hell and anyway he no longer owned a suit, came in full regalia, light blue shirt over dark blue pants with the gold stripe down the legs, dark blue tie, and the original babe magnet, his Smokey hat to top off the ensemble. He left the utility belt at home and the sidearm in the glove compartment.

"You're strutting," Wy said when he came out of the bedroom.

"Nonsense," he said, and squared away his tie.

Sybilla's was a surprisingly pleasant room, spacious with a large window that actually opened. It was stuffed with old-fashioned furniture and knickknacks. The walls were covered with photographs, including several studio portraits of Sybilla in her various primes.

"You look like a movie star, Sybilla," Wy said, staring at one of them. The movie-star version was wearing one of those old timey velvet, V-neck dresses barely held up by the shoulders. Sybilla had turned to look directly into the lens of the camera. She was red-lipped and smiling, her brows two straight black slashes, her hair a dusky cloud.

She looked like sex on a stick, Liam thought, but wisely did not say so out loud.

Sybilla chuckled, busying herself with pouring the tea from a pretty flowered teapot into translucent cups that matched. "Yes, I cleaned up pretty well back in the day. You look nice yourselves. Thank you for indulging an old woman by dressing for the occasion. That's a lovely color on you, my dear."

She was in very good form, sparking on all four cylinders. She was fully clothed, today in a black and white dress that made her look like Grace Kelly in *Rear Window*. Again, it was about two sizes too big. She remembered who Wy and Liam were, their names, and that she had invited them for tea. They sat and she served them warm scones with butter and raspberry jam. Wy took the first bite and said with her mouth full, "You can cook, too?"

Sybilla waved an airy hand. "I am a woman of many talents, my dear. And they do allow us kitchen privileges here, thank goodness."

It was a pleasant afternoon, and Sybilla wiled away the time by spinning tales of Alaskans in days gone by, when men were men and women did all the work.

"So like now," Wy said.

Sybilla's eyes sparkled. "Exactly like now, my dear."

Liam, outnumbered, reached for another scone.

Among Sybilla's collection of days gone by was a turntable and a collection of vinyl records. She selected an album by Ella Fitzgerald and put it on. Sybilla's voice was still strong enough to sound good and she kept up with every word and every note of "It Don't Mean a Thing." She laughed at their expressions when the song ended. "By way of establishing my bona fides," she said.

A little later Liam said, "Did you know that Erik Berglund was Sally Petroff's biological father?"

Sybilla looked surprised. "Of course, dear. Erik and Kimberley were both students of mine." She grimaced. "It was pretty obvious, but then it always is. Girls disappear for a semester or a year and there is always some plausible excuse, an exchange student program opportunity out of state, something like that. And then the following year they come back and life goes on." Her face clouded over. "This was different, of course. Erik went Outside to college, and

Kimberley married Alexei and seven months later Sally was born. A few snide remarks were made but—" She shrugged. "There was another scandal, as there always is, and that one was forgotten."

"They were from Kapilat," Wy said. "Why didn't they go to school there?"

"Unfortunately at that time the Kapilat school had fallen beneath the ten-student limit and the state had closed it. Some families went the home schooling route but a few who had relatives in Blewestown they could board their children with sent them here to complete high school. The two were in the band together. Kimberley played the clarinet and Erik the saxophone." She looked down at her hands and said softly, "I feel responsible. I paired them up on that duet. Benny Goodman, you know. And of course Kimberley's parents would never have let them marry." She saw their mystified looks. "He wasn't Native, you see, and her parents were very traditional. Much like Alexei's family." She sighed. "Which was probably why she chose him."

Wy could feel Liam looking at her. She knew he was remembering her insistence on a small wedding, Bill to officiate, Moses to give her away, two random witnesses they'd pulled off their stools at the bar. None of Wy's blood relatives from Ik'iki'ka. "Did Alexei know?" she said.

"I don't know. I wondered at the time. But Kimberley was smart and capable and a true beauty, quite the catch. He might have known and not have cared."

Toward the end of the visit, Liam and Wy exchanged a

glance, and Wy said, "We were so sorry to hear about your brother Hilary."

"Who?" Sybilla said vaguely, and for a moment Liam thought she was going to phase from one reality to another. He looked around and spotted a robe lying on her bed. Just in case. And then Sybilla's eyes sharpened into the now and she said, "Oh yes, Hilary. Well, my dears, I appreciate the sentiment but Hilary and I were never close."

"What a shame," Wy murmured.

"Yes, well, he was a bit of a prude, my brother. He did not approve of either my job or my lifestyle, I'm afraid."

"He didn't like you singing?"

"Not singing or slinging liquor, either," Sybilla said cheerfully. "Although to be fair, his dislike of my owning a bar might have had something to do with his intolerance for alcohol. It wasn't as if he could partake himself, you see."

There was a pause. "His intolerance for alcohol?" Liam said.

"You mean like allergic?" Wy said.

"Oh my yes," Sybilla said, "acutely. We found out when we were teenagers. The two of us were at a party at a friend's house and his parents weren't home so of course we got into the liquor cabinet. After one drink Hilary started vomiting and his blood pressure dropped so low and so fast that he actually fainted. No, he never touched liquor, my brother."

"Who else knew this, Sybilla?" Liam said in a voice that sounded strange to his own ears.

She shrugged. "Myself, a few close friends. It wasn't

something he talked about." She reflected. "The fainting incident didn't do his social life any good afterward, I'm afraid. The other kids nicknamed him the Dying Swan and he was incapable of laughing it off, so he carried that all the rest of the way through high school. I think he went to college out of state to get away from it. And then, when he did come home, the arthritis kicked in. He was three years younger than I was and he looked thirty years older."

Illness might have had that effect, Liam thought.

So might guilt.

"Poor Hilary," Sybilla said. "He never really had a chance at life, you know? I'm certain he died a virgin."

She looked up to see them staring at her. "What?"

Acknowledgments

ALL MY GRATITUDE GOES TO BARBARA Peters and Nic Cheetham, who never beat up on me for being first one, and then two, and then three, and now four months over deadline. The price of an understanding editor and publisher is far above rubies. The title of my next work is going to be *Love and Not Writing in the Time of Covid-19*.

Astute readers will notice the geographic similarities between the real life Kachemak Bay and the wholly imaginary Chungasqak Bay. Liam's new post was inspired by but not based on the real thing, in much the same way his old post of Newenham was inspired by but not based on Dillingham. It is, you might say, a distinction with a difference, and in this case a whole lot of differences, beginning with place names. I love true local place names and many of the names herein were found in online dictionaries like Liicugtukut Alutiit'stun. By all accounts the old folks were practical people and if there was a bay where the blueberries grew especially well I'm betting they would have called such a place Blueberry Bay, so I did, too.

Oil companies were run out of Kachemak Bay decades ago, mostly due to their own ineptitude. Chungasqak Bay, not so much. I mean it to be a fictional reflection of the eternal Alaskan fight between maintaining the natural resources that have nourished Alaskans for millennia and the commercial extraction of fossil fuels and precious minerals that provide jobs and the state taxes that pay to fix potholes. If you want to start a fight, stand on a street corner anywhere in Alaska and take one side or the other.

The bits and pieces found by the archeologist were inspired by Janet R. Klein's 'The Fort Kenai Collection,' collected in *150 Years: Proceedings of the 2017 Kenai Peninsula History Conference*. Klein has written a lot about history and archeology in Alaska, including *Archeology in Alaska* and *Kachemak Bay Communities: Their Histories, Their Mysteries*, and with her daughter co-authored a children's book called *Alaska Dinosaurs and other Cretaceous Creatures*. It doubles as a coloring book, and the icon for carnivore is hilarious. My recommendation for any kid's next birthday present. You're welcome.

About the author

DANA STABENOW was born in Anchorage, Alaska and raised on a 75-foot fishing tender. She knew there was a warmer, drier job out there somewhere and found it in writing. Her first Kate Shugak book, *A Cold Day for Murder*, received an Edgar Award from the Crime Writers of America. Find her online at stabenow.com

LIAM CAMPBELL INVESTIGATIONS

KATE SHUGAK INVESTIGATIONS